Edward & The Wilderness

By Charles Martin & Will Weinke

Edited by Emily Jerman & Kristen Grace.

Lettering by Ashley Couch.

Layout and Design by April Marciszewski and Charles J. Martin.

Edward and the Island Copyright © 2010 by Charles Martin.

Edward and the Island Copyright © 2017 by Charles Martin.

Edward and the Wilderness Copyright © 2017 by Charles Martin.

Edward & The Wilderness

By Charles Martin & Will Weinke

LITERATI PRESS
COMICS LP NOVELS
BOOKSHOP & COMMUNITY

Note to the reader:

In spite of it all, we must find a place for hope.

—Bali

I Cannot Die
Part 1

Tumbling toward the outer rim of God's realm, I remember love distantly, like the lingering, sour burn of cheap whiskey. I am alone among the stars, cast away from the Island, abandoned by my Father. Again. Steadily falling toward the end of the universe, I am approaching the threshold where even God does not dare travel.

I do not possess a ship. It's only me, the vacuum, momentum, and immortality. I send these words to you because I believe that you can hear them. It has been so long since we've spoken, but I can now feel your attention like the subtle rise and fall of barometric pressure as spring storms sweep across the horizon, whispering their empty threats.

You are growing stronger, aren't you? That is why I now sense your presence for the first time in—exactly how long has it been? I cannot perceive time anymore. Days, weeks, years—they no longer exist for me. Space only gives way to more space as I am propelled forward by God's fury. We are all drifting toward nothingness, of course, but I am moving at a brisker clip.

Yet time hasn't extinguished my memories. If anything, the empty space has forced me to live within my mind, the negative relief bringing my thoughts vividly to the foreground. The eternal silence washed away the walls that stood between my past and my present. Voices from long ago cushion me from the vacuum and are my only company on this long, aimless journey.

But what a life I've lived!

So many people I've loved. On Earth, I enlightened the Chosen People, I commanded great armies, seduced artists, philosophers, and kings. I was humanity's closest, most loyal friend. On the Island, I offered myself as their greatest sacrifice. Even the King of Kings owes His survival to me, His greatest rival, the Second Son of God. When all of Creation came within a breath of destruction, I was the one who pulled God and all His bright and beautiful creatures from the precipice.

I am your Savior. I am the one who truly loved you. I am your Antichrist. I am Bali.

The Island

The end of Earth came and went. The Judgment Day, the ascent to Heaven, and the descent to Hell. Our places settled. Whether damned or saved, we were no longer wanderers in God's lonely universe.

Then we began waking, old souls bound to young human bodies, transported to an island held aloft by God's will. We overlooked the Kingdom, the living fabric of Heaven. The Island was forested and blessed by a grand lake separating two land masses which resembled Earth, but were artifices, homages. The differences were subtle at first, but children are curious creatures. They found the seams of this new reality quickly. Humanity: Creation's greatest exploiter.

On one side of the Island, God placed a cluster of cabins, a mess hall, metal sheds, and a landing strip. On the other, an impenetrable canopy of trees forbidden to the children. I was the lone ambassador who traveled freely from one side to the other. A guest in all homes, yet belonging to none. Just as it had always been.

In the campground we found God personified, a forgettable and distant middle-aged man who wore His new flesh awkwardly—a father trying, and failing, to fit in with his children. He knew everything about humanity, its entire history, its darkest secrets, yet He understood so little. But that is why He created Earth—to understand. The experiment failed to enlighten God on the mystery of free will. So He created the Island, a second, smaller experiment to dissect the minds and motivations of His chosen people.

God's campground was similar to thousands of Christian retreats spread throughout North America in the 21st century. The souls originated, for the most part, from that same time and place. During the final age of mankind. This was for, as God stated, "simplicity's sake."

I was an exception. I have existed in many forms throughout time. Jay was also an exception. On Earth, he was Jesus of Nazareth, but God decided to hide His son's identity for, as God stated, "simplicity's sake."

I have never met a being as conflicted as Jay. So sad and bitter, endlessly haunted by the terrible burden his father placed on him. The Island physically pained him. Even the slightest touch of water reopened the wounds of his crucifixion, letting his sacred blood flow. Jay was poorly adapted to the Island, and the Island was poorly adapted to the children, and God was poorly adapted to everything else. Unlike the elegant genius of evolution that crafted Earth, the Island was a rushed project, a rogue idea from a bored Creator just wanting to get His hands dirty again.

Jay and I were created as teenage twins expected to oversee herds of children brought to the Island. I was the advocate for the humans and Jay was the voice of God, just as we'd been on Earth.

I kept records and was gifted with the ability to see into the minds of all those on the Island. Aside from God.

Jay enforced God's law with the help of an army of invisible angels.

The human souls were returned to their childhood bodies, but Jay and I appeared to be teenagers. God assumed that our taller stature and illusion of age would give us a natural authority over the children. He wanted the humans to toe the line immediately.

Some did, some did not.

When the children failed to meet God's standard, they were exiled to the other side of the Island and maturity cast upon them like a plague. Once the campground emptied out and all its former inhabitants had become adult castaways, God would cull another herd from Heaven. These children would never be told of those that had come before.

Eventually, Edward and his group arrived. I never knew what curiosity God satiated with the Island experiment, but Edward's arrival marked a turning point. God would soon lose control of His creation. The endurance of the human spirit would finally overwhelm the throne.

But God was also not the same on the Island. As the children found the Island strengthened their abilities, it weakened God's. It would eventually be Edward, the former holy man, who stood over God preparing to murder the Father he'd spent his earthly life trying to love and understand.

Of all those who had tried in the past, it turned out to be a clever, sweet-natured priest who dethroned our Father.

Edward the Fallen

Edward woke as the sun crested the horizon. He was alone.

Even from across the lake, I could feel dread clouding his mind as he gathered supplies and fumbled with the laces of his shoes. He knew it was time to seek out the only person he'd ever loved. Tommy, the beautiful man with eyes always on the water and a restless heart with no patience for home.

"It's okay," Edward's mother often told him when discussing Edward's distant, passionless father. "I have broad shoulders."

After watching his mother suffer for so long, Edward vowed to never fall into a loveless marriage. Since arriving to the Wilderness, Edward had never wanted for passion with Tommy. At night, Edward felt adored, embraced wholly and without reservation. But then morning would come, as it always does, and life would change, as it always does.

Yes, Tommy possessed passion. He burned with it. But devotion?

Three months after his exile from the campground, Edward had yet to wander beyond the shores of the lake and into the Wilderness. Tommy told him to stay near the lake, so he did. Edward's father had also demanded his wife submit to a domestic life. He did find comfort in being protected and coveted and felt he understood his mother a little better for it. But unlike Tommy, Edward's father stayed.

Edward soon found his union with Tommy to be an unwieldy burden, too large and too feral to carry for more than a few hours at a time. This was the lone subject they always, silently agreed upon. This was why Tommy left every morning without a word, but granting one brief, relieved kiss.

Fighting. There was too much fighting. They battled over boundaries they'd never had to set before.

And this was why Edward didn't mind being abandoned every day. He enjoyed the solitude and the time it gave him to adjust to a new reality where God's love was a matter of regret, not faith. God's love existed in its own way. Edward understood this to be true, but a vague idea of love was not enough. It was not what Edward deserved.

Tommy's expeditions began stretching on for longer periods of time. When gone all night, Tommy would struggle back to the shore just as Edward stirred awake. Tommy would be flushed with fever, shaking, muttering nonsense before collapsing to sleep. Edward would fret, but Tommy always recovered. They never discussed Tommy's disappearances. Edward knew that nothing good would come of prying. Another thing he'd learned from his mother.

Once he disappeared for three days and returned with a pleasant smile as if he'd only been gone for the afternoon.

Six days had passed since Tommy had last adventured off into the Wilderness and he had not come home. Edward was ashamed he'd waited for so long, but he was not naive. He understood the behavior; he'd seen it in countless lost souls.

With only a full canteen and two peanut butter sandwiches, Edward struck out on a mission to find his love and bring him back, no matter what state he was in when Edward found him.

"I have broad shoulders," Edward told himself, feeling more familiar with the heaviness of love, like a horse finally accepting the harness.

***

Edward came upon a quiet fishing village not quite a quarter mile down the shoreline. The men sipped from crude bottles and leaned against half-finished shacks with thatched roofs. Of all the minds I visited to keep tabs on the Island, I found the fishers the most distasteful. Even from across the lake, I felt their listless apathy swirling with an inebriated malaise. They drank to ignore the shattered sighs of women gazing out across the waves for the distant death forever lingering across the lake.

In Cabin One. Where God lived.

The villagers were beautiful. But everyone in the Wilderness was beautiful and well-fed. The Island was bountiful in all things except hope.

A dark cluster of trees hid the shacks in their shadows, and thick vegetation covered three aged, hand-carved canoes. Edward had seen the canoes out on the lake, but only late at night when they could safely fish by moonlight, veiled from the curious and frightened eyes of children still held within the Creator's campground.

It was the way of the Wilderness—to live and die just out of view.

Each of God's orphans took to this life differently. Some became lost and angry, others shielded themselves with fatalistic apathy, and a few embraced the Wilderness as a new Manifest Destiny.

These were the ones Tommy feared most.

"Stay out of the forest," he warned Edward the night of his exile. Edward obeyed as long as he could, but six days is too long.

Yet, he also questioned whether he should seek out his lover. Not because he was afraid of the Wilderness, but rather he feared the cycle of pain Tommy represented. He'd counseled enough broken couples to recognize the symptoms. Now, within the midst of his own broken relationship, he felt their sick loneliness. Tommy would never change, but still Edward searched for him.

Faces turned toward Edward as he walked through the fishermen's village. A few of them craned their necks to see if there was anyone else coming behind Edward.

"They come in groups," Tommy had once told Edward.

"Who?"

"It doesn't matter. If people come for you, run. Don't question, don't fight, don't even try to find me. Just run."

Whatever threat Tommy had been warning him about, Edward knew these fishermen were not it. He could tell they were as frightened as Tommy had been. Once they realized Edward was alone, most of them lost interest and sagged back into their familiar ruts.

A thin young woman rose reluctantly from the shore. She shook the sand from her sheer skirt. When she met Edward's eyes, she did so warily, measuring him as if he was an unleashed dog. She walked toward him wearing a disaffected frown in the style of jaded American youth. "Switchblade women," one of Edward's seminary professors had once called them in a tone that conveyed both warning and worship that was common among the celibate. All these years later, Edward recalled the man's words verbatim. "Pearled handles, deadly swishes, an indiscriminate vitriol aimed at the world that doesn't deserve them."

Edward imagined that the young woman had been shaped by God on a lonely adolescent night. Her rail-thin waist stretched up to curves almost too generous to be feasible. It seemed a soft wind could snap her at the waist, splintering her spine like a matchstick in a shivering hand.

Her smooth skin and cold, angular face reminded Edward of the kind of woman he would have tried to dream of when he still thought he had a chance at a normal life. That was before he gave up trying to redirect his sexuality and opted for "undeclared."

"Finally straying from your beach house?" the woman asked Edward as she neared. He was troubled by the implication that they'd been watching him, but he let it pass.

"I'm looking for a man named Tommy," Edward said. "Blond hair, tall ..."

"We know Tommy," the woman said.

A few chuckles bubbled up from the fishermen. She smiled.

"You're the gay pastor—Eddy, right?"

It was what Tommy called him. Only Tommy. It pierced like a betrayal to hear the nickname slide so easily from her mouth.

His stomach twisted with premonition. "Where is he?"

"Breaking your heart."

Edward turned his face to the forest so she wouldn't see the tear that broke through. The switchblade woman smiled, satisfied, then returned to the shore and sat down on the sand.

The soft wind exchanged hushed gossip with the trees.

Murmurs from the fishermen brought his attention around. They watched the lake, standing and shielding their eyes from the morning sun peering over the shoulder of the campground. Edward squinted through the glare and found a dozen black dots on the water.

"That must be all of them," one of the men said. Then he turned to Edward. "Never seen so many all at the same time. God must be having a bad day."

"God's always having a bad day," the switchblade woman said, inspiring a lively rumble of laughter from everyone but Edward, who was already sprinting back toward his campground.

Edward the Fallen
Part 2

Rowboats were inching across the vast lake toward Edward as he arrived at the shoreline near his campground. He cast a hopeful glance toward the trees where Tommy's tent was set up. Tommy was still gone.

He turned back to peer across the water, then up at the sun beaming down from the center of the sky. On Earth, the sun's rhythm was certain enough to build life around. On the Island, God instead lobbed the sun across the horizon at His whim as part of a cruel, teasing dance that drove some of the weaker exiles mad.

As the rowboats approached, Edward was reminded of watching sailboats return to shore.

"They look like they are rising from the water because of the curvature of the Earth," his father had told him. "That is how we know the world is round."

"But people used to believe the world was flat when we had boats," Edward replied.

"Yes, for quite a long time."

"How could people be so stupid for so long?" Edward asked.

"Because we can only spy through a keyhole, my boy. We do the best we can. Only through God can we open the door and see the world for what it really is."

There was no curvature on the Island. This world really was flat, as if God had pulled up a slab of soil and tossed it into space. And there was God, only a boat ride away. In Edward's former life as a pastor, he never imagined being so close to the Creator. Yet he had never felt so separated and alone.

"I have touched the body of Christ," Edward prayed on his

first night in the Wilderness. "I have heard Him talk and seen Him for what He truly is. How could I have been so stupid for so long?"

As Edward waited for the rowboats, tears rose to his eyes. With isolation, Edward had embraced the cleansing act of crying. He wept without shame, especially in Tommy's absence, as if trying to sweat out a fever. With enough tears, he thought the love might eventually seep out too—and with it, the pain.

A figure stood in the lead boat, tall, and lean. Assured. Billy.

Edward waved. Billy waved back, then sat down to retake the oars.

Two boats separated from the group, listing toward another patch of shoreline. Edward guessed it was Martha and her fanatical friends, seeking out their Plymouth Rock where they could establish a more perfect union.

With the boats closing in, Edward could see faces he recognized, still familiar even after maturing into adulthood. Among them were his friends:

Me—the guide,

Billy—the soldier,

Sophia—the nun,

Todd—the lawyer,

Raul—the guitar player,

Ossie—the man Edward wanted to be.

And, somewhere within the Wilderness, were the friends already exiled:

Petrov—the artist,

Barry and Mary—the unabashed lovers,

Tommy—the man Edward couldn't escape.

But no Simon. Edward scanned the boats a second time

as they approached, searching for the former Vegas magician who had lost his fear of God, yet was never exiled from the campground. Simon would not be broken, not like the others, and perhaps that is exactly why God held the boy so close.

Or perhaps Simon was dead.

Or perhaps the boy had performed the greatest magic trick of all and escaped God.

Billy the Warrior

By the end, Billy fought to stay in the campground in much the same way he had fought to salvage his marriage back on Earth. There was no joy, there was no hope. There was only the familiar, but that was enough to stay and suffer.

Once Simon disappeared, God seemed to disengage from the children, spending most of His time hidden away in the cabin. He built His miniature battlefields with tiny, living statues, disregarding real humans for something more false and pliable. Even Jay would be left standing dumbly at the cabin door, knocking, avoiding the eyes of amused campers watching the Creator's only son facing the same baffling silence humans had endured since they possessed the language to plead to God for mercy.

The fever of growth swept across the remaining campers overnight. Dozens of children sprouted to adulthood in seven agonizing hours, waking to their waiting God. He wore a black funeral suit, black dress socks, and pale blue hospital slippers while gazing across the shore with pupiless eyes kept hidden behind soft brown sunglasses.

The campers, soon to be exiles, were allowed to eat one last meal in the mess hall before they were to assemble at the shore. Brand-new rowboats were crowded along the small dock, clacking into one another with the gentle waves.

"I know that many of you are scared," I told the campers as they listlessly ate. "I know that some of you are eager to leave. Regardless, I will be there with you. I will make my way across the lake to check up on you as often as I can manage. However you may feel about your time on the Island, you have not and will not be abandoned. You will have me and you will have each other."

"God is challenging us," Martha called from her group's table in the back of the mess hall. The five women were still clothed in their white improvised burkas, now too small to cover their legs. Blond and brown hairs sprouted from their pale, pink shins , like the first weeds of spring.

"We do not need you, Bali," she continued. "We need only God."

"Yes, that's good," I encouraged her. "Hold your faith in any way you can. Though we'll no longer be protecting you from the elements, feeding you, or dictating your behavior, hope is not lost. Life can be found in the Wilderness. It is dangerous, it's not to be taken lightly, but for those willing to work hard and believe, amazing things are possible. Things you could've never imagined on Earth, or even here in the campground."

Though meant to be encouraging, my words instead inspired a few soft whimpers and eyes hardened by grim panic. Fantastical worlds were only exciting in movies and books, where readers could hide comfortably behind the fourth wall.

It was the same deep unease Billy had felt on the bus ride to Paris Island where he would become a Marine. But this time he was not alone, and that intensified his nervousness into a hot, twisting nausea inside his gut.

His eyes trailed across the mess hall to the table where Sophia sat, her legs long and smooth, her curves subtle but feminine. Testosterone raged within Billy now, his body fully awake to the possibilities of adulthood. Eager. Hungry. The intoxicating conqueror's spirit that drove him into war now commanded that he rip away God's reins and take control of his own life.

And take Sophia with him.

Fear did not make Billy wilt, as it did the others. It enraged him.

"Where is Simon?" Billy called.

"I don't know," I responded.

"Where is Edward and Petrov? Barry and Mary, all the others who were sent over?"

I glanced behind him toward a window looking out to God's cabin.

"Once we have made our way to the Wilderness," I said carefully, "I will answer as many of your questions as I can."

Billy tossed his fork onto his tray. He pushed away from the table and strode for the door. Ossie looked to Sophia and nodded for her to follow Billy while Ossie collected Billy's tray.

Ossie believed in the value of leaving on good terms, whether an employer, a lover, or a god.

***

The height disparity was striking as Billy stood next to God. Billy, a towering, broad-shouldered man, made the Creator look squat, soft, old, and feeble. They both watched the water from the edge of the pier as Sophia approached. If they were speaking, she couldn't hear it.

Billy turned just enough to eye Sophia approaching, his face cold, his anger reserved but very present. He turned back to the water and Sophia kept her distance.

In time, the rest of the campers joined Sophia. They crowded around the pier, unsure and hoping for answers.

"Excuse me, everyone," I called. All but Billy and God turned to face me as I stood before them. "Return to your cabins. There are backpacks prepared for all of you on your bunks. Get them, then return here. We will leave together. Do you understand?"

No one replied. They dispersed with only a few whispers as I motioned to Ossie.

"Get Billy's backpack too, please."

Ossie nodded. Billy still had not turned from the water, had not moved from God's side.

I walked to the rowboats and mentally arranged the campers inside, ensuring at least one competent rower per boat. Martha's horde would be stuffed into two boats, whether or not they had the ability to navigate across the lake. They could fall off the side of the Island, for all I cared.

The image played out in my mind, the burka-clad cultists surging toward the lake's waterfall, manically paddling against the current before toppling over the side of the Island like a spilled laundry basket of screaming bedsheets.

I chuckled, which brought an almost imperceptible huff from God. I was interrupting the silent game raging between Him and Billy.

The campers returned quickly and I pointed them to their assigned spots, the strongest manning the oars, the rest placed to avoid personality conflicts and/or scheming. I'd never taken so many over at one time, so mutiny seemed a viable threat.

"Billy," I whispered. "It's time."

Billy didn't respond at first. Seconds passed and I waited. Billy swiveled to face God, whose eyes still had not wavered from the water. Billy leaned closer, his nose only a few inches from the stoic Creator's.

"Billy," I said, a soft warning.

Billy turned abruptly, bumping his shoulder against God's and throwing Him off balance. God took a half step backwards and watched Billy storm past me. As Billy stepped down into a boat, God's eyes moved to mine. I shook my head. God's focus returned to the lake, His scowl deeply set, but His wrath subdued.

For now.

Sister Sophia

The priest took her passport. That was how it started. That was when she should have known.

"Run home!" Sophia screamed in her mind as her face masked the fear with a tense smile.

"It is for your protection," the priest insisted.

"Of course," Sophia replied. Obedience in the name of God. Her greatest virtue, what her mother stressed above all things, what the priest saw when he handpicked her to help reach the desperate and unredeemed trapped within the darkest corners of Africa.

"Don't say his name," echoed in Sophia's mind, a mantra to pull her out of her memories and back to the Island. "Don't say his name. Don't say his name."

The priest died when the world ended, Sophia reminded herself. He was in Hell now. He must be. Don't say his name and he stays dead. He never exists again.

Beyond the water was the Wilderness, a dense tangle of trees and mystery. She thought of the village, the priest, the men.

"Don't say his name."

"Sophia," Billy whispered. "I'm here. It will be okay."

"I know," Sophia answered, her eyes shut tight, squeezing out the nightmare.

She focused on the sounds of the oars dipping into the water, sloshing, squeaking as they lifted, moved forward, and dropped into the lake again. Her fingertips found the cool water rushing by the boat.

"Don't say his name," Sophia demanded, this time out loud to hear her own voice.

Billy knew not to respond. He understood how terror worked. If Ossie heard, he didn't let on.

A sickly flush rose to her face. Her heart seized like a clinched hose, then released with a hard thump. Again. Again. Again. Perspiration rose to her skin. She smelled the priest's cheap cologne, felt the filth of his basement sticking to her skin, fighting its way inside her soul.

"Don't say his name."

A soft, tiny bite on her fingertips. Sophia's eyes shot open as her hand jerked out of the water.

"What?" Billy asked, but Sophia didn't answer, turning her focus to the water. From all around the boat, dark shadows swam toward the hull. The other exiles stopped paddling and watched as thousands of fish wound their way toward, beneath, and around Sophia's boat.

Sophia gazed down into the water, watching the flurry of activity.

"Shit," Billy grunted, lifting the oars out of the water. Ossie edged toward the center of the boat.

"It's okay," Sophia gasped, tears dropping from her cheeks, dripping down into the water. "It's okay."

Sophia looked to Billy, a smile beaming on her face.

"It's okay," she repeated.

Sophia reached to the water, softly touching a massive catfish swimming alongside the drifting boat like a curious dog. It kept pace with the boat as she stroked its slick skin.

She looked to the distant shore ahead. She wiped the tears with the back of her hand.

"Okay," she said. "Let's go."

Billy lowered the oars back into the water. As they dipped under the surface, the fish fanned out on both sides, escorting Sophia onward.

Low, quick thrumming brought Sophia's eyes to squadrons of dragonflies approaching from the Wilderness, zipping just above the water, sweeping in front of the boat in jittery darts as they held a sort of protective formation at the bow of the rowboat.

"Look!" Ossie called, pointing to the shore where a lone figure stood, watching.

Billy turned in his seat, then stood. The figure waved.

"I'll be damned," Billy grunted. "I think that's Edward."

Billy returned the wave, then sat back down and took to the oars. He looked into Sophia's face as she watched the busy dragonflies. She let her eyes settle on Billy. She gave an optimistic sigh, tears still dripping. She wiped them away.

"I hate bugs," Billy said. Sophia laughed. She leaned over and pecked a kiss on his lips.

"Onward, Jeeves," Sophia announced, waving the boat forward.

"As you wish," Billy replied, pulling the oars to his chest, the boat gently lurching forward toward the Wilderness.

The Engineers

Mildred Zimer had not concealed her aged and wrinkled body for several years. The determined nudist embraced the spots, the sags, and the rolls of the mature human form. Most exiles would never allow their bodies to age past the Earth equivalent of 21, but Mildred's clock was whirring well beyond the ripeness of young adulthood and past the outer edges of menopause.

She considered clothes a meaningless relic of a long-dead world. Mildred was an Engineer, perhaps the boldest of them all.

And the fastest. She darted through the forest with the grace and speed of a panther. She ran with inexhaustible joy, her folds and bulges dancing with the movement. Her bright, gray-toothed smile beaming. On this latest hunt, she kept her green eyes steady on the young man sprinting out ahead of her.

She would overtake him when she thought it was time. She was relishing the chase, the dominance, the control.

But she had not always been like this.

On Earth, it took a case of crabs to finally convince Mildred that her husband would never shirk off his devotion to his timid little prostitute. For all Mildred knew, the young girl could have been homeless. On several occasions over the course of seven years, Mildred had followed her husband into the city, exiting off the highway in the part of town that white people only visited if they were up to no good. She would follow his taillights as they wound through a dense apartment block where the girl would be sitting by a dumpster, freezing, emaciated, dying slowly like a domesticated pet that had been abandoned with no ability to care for itself.

Mildred pitied the girl and, despite the humiliation and pain, Mildred pitied her husband too. It started after the death of their youngest daughter. It was all related, somehow, in that twisted way pain and love warp everything. In time, Mildred realized that she couldn't stay. In the following years, their surviving daughter, Ailey, would come to despise Mildred. The vile things the child said: Mildred deserving a cheating husband, being too ugly to be wanted, being too weak to love. Mildred didn't know what else to do but absorb her daughter's fury and hope things would change.

After Ailey graduated from high school, Mildred would never see her again. Her ex-husband would catch Mildred up on their daughter's life, but it all seemed false, a fantasy. Law school? A stable husband and children? One home in Boston, another off the coast of Florida?

Happy?

Ailey would only tell this to the father, but not the woman who raised her, the woman who served as the receptacle for all Aiely's confused vitriol.

It was wrong. It was all wrong. Every bit of Aieley's life was wrong. And Mildred's life as well.

Like a considerate house guest, death arrived promptly for Mildred and without much fuss. A brain aneurysm.

Mildred Zimer didn't toss away her clothes her first day on the Island. She started out frightened and confused, just like everyone else. It took time to realize her potential. She started stretching out her abilities after a few weeks in the campground when she discovered that there was something special about her. Once exiled into the Wilderness, she tested the outer edges of this more flexible physical world. She called herself an Engineer because she felt like she was tinkering with God's loosely defined reality, building with her mind and will in much the same way scientists on Earth built with chemicals, fire, and electricity. Other exiles soon joined her, exploring their own special abilities while poking and prodding at the Island's relative physics.

And Mildred began collecting lovers. No more monogamy. At the time of Edward's arrival on the Island, she had four lovers, both male and female, each serving a different purpose. Customized romances to suit her array of kinks and whimsies.

Two of these lovers were technically prostitutes. She was beginning to understand her ex-husband.

Her withered body was a mark of an Engineer. The most powerful of the exiles, Engineers embraced age as a sign of enlightenment. In Mildred's mind, her aged body was the most beautiful it had ever been. Like a weathered mountain range, sculpted by time, it showed the passage of ages.

Endurance. That was what it took to be great in the Wilderness.

Mildred closed the distance between her and her prey—a young, broad-shouldered man named Jonathan. His pace was slowing, his skin was flushed, he was stumbling. Mildred laughed at the man, taunting him.

Jonathan turned from the forest into a clearing, staggering forward and falling to the grass. With the edge of the Island on one side and an Engineer on the other, he was trapped. Mildred slowed and stood before him.

Jonathan was a rapist from America. He started running the instant he saw Mildred approach from the forests north of New Wichita. The chase tore through three miles of dense vegetation and across two streams. Jonathan had sprinted with every spark of energy his body could afford, yet Mildred was always two steps behind.

Mildred's breath was even, as if she was at the end of a leisurely stroll. She was, after all, an Engineer.

"Please!" the young man begged, hands held up defensively. "I can explain."

"Of course you can," Mildred replied with a warm smile. "I

am here to help."

Jonathan pushed to his feet and backed away. Just a few feet of land separated him from the fall into the fabric of Heaven.

"What was her name?" Mildred asked.

"It was a misunderstanding," the man said, still inching backwards, bracing for a blow.

"What was her name?" Mildred repeated, her smile unwavering. Mildred was anxious to settle this business so she could return to the rest of the Engineers to discuss how to handle Edward. But she also loved to play with the guilty. She loved watching them twist and wiggle, worms on fishing hooks.

Jonathan took his time considering his answer, drew in a deep breath, and let his eyes fall to the ground.

"Emily."

"I don't know Emily," Mildred said. "I hadn't met her before today when she came asking for my help. Is she lying?"

"Yes! She is confused! I shouldn't have slept with her, I knew how she was. You know—off. It was a mistake and I am sorry, but I didn't rape her."

Mildred glanced down to Jonathan's feet, now inches from the edge.

"Be careful," Mildred said. "You don't want to fall."

The ground cracked and split. The grass crumbled beneath him. He flailed his arms to regain his balance, almost tipping off the edge of the Island. A three-foot section of ground split away, with Jonathan on it, and drifted away from the edge of the Island. Jonathan prepared to leap back.

"No!" Mildred screamed, her voice unnaturally shrill.

Jonathan nearly fell from the floating slab. He settled and looked at Mildred with pleading eyes. Mildred's frown softened to a smile.

"You will stay put," she said.

Jonathan continued drifting away from the Island. The slab finally stopped twenty feet from the edge, hovering in place.

"Please don't do this!" Jonathan yelled.

The slab began disintegrating around him, its soil falling along the underside of the Island, down into the ocean of souls winding in the living sea of Heaven. Thousands upon thousands of tiny threads, knitting themselves during their perpetual slumber within Paradise.

Jonathan was left with just one square foot of soil holding him aloft. He stood upright, at attention, terrified.

"You can't leave me like this," Jonathan whimpered.

"I will return for you," Mildred replied, turning back to the forest. "Probably."

"I can't stay like this! I'm going to fall!" Jonathan kept his eyes level and his arms out wide like a tightrope walker.

"Perhaps."

"Engineer!" Jonathan called.

Mildred sighed and turned to face the man.

"What happens if I fall?"

"I have no idea," Mildred answered, displaying a wry, crooked-toothed smile. "But God can't catch you. Not here, not on this side of the Island."

"Of course he can catch me! God can do anything!"

"Only if we let Him."

I Cannot Die
Part 2

I was born a bastard, the shameful son of God, a secret hidden among the ranks of angels. I did not understand my true origin until the heralded arrival of Adam.

They called me the "Morning Star" because I was the brightest of all the angels. Only My Father and I knew the truth. I was of God, not merely created by Him. It is a difficult distinction to explain and even more difficult to accept once God told me how I fit into His plan for mankind.

The Tempter.

You see, humans are a terrible creation. They are slow and awkward, with soft flesh and not a single effective weapon inherent in their frame.

Aside from their minds.

Upon their creation, Adam and his multitude fled to the water, shivering in the waves, too afraid of the great land beasts to crawl to shore and begin fulfilling God's weighty expectations.

I was sent to Adam to spark his mind to life, to extinguish the fear and replace it with wrath, greed, pride, lust, and envy. Sin did not exist in spite of God; He created it to overwhelm man's base instinct for survival, to offset his physical weakness by igniting their intellectual brilliance.

This was why I was created, to shepherd my distant kin into the wilderness of Earth and, through their minds, dominate it.

But now I have been ejected from God's plan and on my journey toward oblivion, I have witnessed planets that teem with life. Near Earths so like the beautiful blue planet we once called home. But these were still vital, young, but so fragile. I often wondered what role God's hand played in these worlds.

I know many things, have served witness to God's greatest wonders and peered into His deepest mysteries.

But I cannot say if there are other chosen people toiling away on the millions of living orbs spread across the great expanse. Even in Heaven and Hell, there are curtains obscuring portions of God's plan.

Like any dismayed child wondering about an absent father, I could only hope that all His heart was directed toward me.

Even the suns in the outermost galaxies have now faded to glimmering pinpricks as I race beyond the outward sprawl of the universe. The Wall nears. Few have seen it, none have passed through it. The Wall was a curiosity for the more adventurous of us during the early time of the universe. Beyond The Wall means beyond God, beyond His Creation, beyond His Light.

Of course, I've been severed from Divinity before, as punishment for our failed rebellion. It was a different kind of darkness. A darkness within God instead of without, but a darkness all the same. After returning from Hell, I could never enjoy Earth's winters. It was the chill that brought me low.

Theologians believed that my fall from grace came when I refused to bow before man, but they are wrong. I loved mankind. I have always felt protective of the human race. I was just as eager as God to see them grow into their dominion.

I turned from God when He told me that my own brother would be placed above me, not only in His kingdom, but within the hearts of men. My secret brother. The favored and, to my mind, the undeserving Son of God.

So I resisted. I rebelled. I lost. In the coming millennia of humanity's rule over Earth, I loved you all and guided your minds the best I could while my brother courted your hearts.

He helped you forgive; I helped you overcome. You worshiped him and reviled me.

And now, with The Wall so close, I believe I have finally forgiven you.

Martha the Believer

Faith was always a sort of game to Martha. Her family suffered a poverty that most people of her time didn't think existed. People imagined poverty as urban blight, drug dealers, and towering apartment blocks.

They never thought of Elma, South Dakota.

Martha didn't experience indoor plumbing until she visited her grandfather in the hospital. Only five at the time, Martha refused to flush the toilet. She didn't care how cross her mother became. It seemed unnaturally intense.

Martha lost two siblings to the brutal South Dakota winters. Homemade quilts and a modest wood-burning stove were not enough to stave off death's icy grasp. The father left shortly after the second boy passed, unable to coexist with a "house full of ugly heifers." Martha didn't understand what her father meant until years later, when the poor girl became aware that she was what her mother delicately called "a little on the sturdy side."

Martha's mother feared God only slightly more than she feared the Crow Indians, whose reservation sat not far from town.

"We are defenseless," Martha's mother would say while in the midst of one of her spells. During these frightful times, the frail woman would block the front door, close all the curtains, and retreat to bed with a kitchen knife and a shotgun. She wouldn't rise from bed for days, leaving Martha to wander the countryside to knock at distant doors, hoping to find charity.

One elderly man did, from time to time, take an interest in Martha's upbringing. He took her to the church where she would eventually come to peace with her fear of indoor plumbing. Those Sunday mornings at church were happy times for Martha. Like school, church meant a reprieve from her emotionally brittle mother. But church didn't torment Martha with tests and bullies. All Martha had to do was listen and believe.

"We are His warriors, and we must all find our place on the battlefield," the brooding preacher announced, glowering at the parishioners.

Most found the young preacher's fervor unnerving, but Martha took comfort in his unwavering conviction. In his words, life seemed so much simpler, so much more certain. Clarity was not an easy thing to come by in Elma, so the preacher's rigid definitions of life were attractive to the confused, scared, and lost little girl.

The preacher was a thin, reedy man with deep-set eyes—not handsome in the traditional sense—but he spoke with a practiced and enlightened diction Martha found enchanting.

She was in love, of course.

Once she asked him how she could be a warrior, how she was expected to start her path out of Elma and on to Paradise. The preacher scribbled out passages of the Bible and sent them home with Martha for her to study before reporting back the next Sunday.

He was her only true advocate.

Her mother once went six days without speaking or eating after a letter had arrived from the county sheriff. Martha would never know what the letter said, but she was certain it had something to do with her wayward father. Martha set out on a ten mile walk into town seeking his help and guidance.

"Childhood is not meant to be enjoyed, but endured," the preacher told her. He then called the police and scrounged up stale sugar wafers leftover from women's bible study. The wafers would be her first meal in two days.

"The devil is behind it all," the preacher whispered to her, so close now that she could smell the chewing tobacco on his breath. "Your faith is your shield here on Earth. In Heaven, God will cleanse all your wounds."

Her heart urged her to fall into his arms, certain that this was the love of her lifetime.

But this, she decided, was another trial of the devil.

I had nothing to do with it, of course.

***

As their boat slid into the mud along the shoreline of the Wilderness, Martha did not feel like a warrior nor did her small group of followers feel like an army. Instead, she was overcome by the same confusion of her early days of faith, desperate for direction as she tried to decipher impenetrable scripture.

"It's pretty," a follower suggested, then was quickly hushed by the others.

Martha lifted the bed sheet burqa to her thighs, struggled out of the boat, and trudged through the water. Her followers, also covered by white sheets and hoods with improvised eye holes, silently followed, pulling the two boats onto the shore. They unloaded the boats and slung the backpacks over their shoulders. A follower brought the last backpack to Martha, who stared at the woods.

"So, we wait for Bali?" the follower asked.

"We don't need Bali," Martha replied, looking along the shoreline. The other boats had landed further up the beach and were met by Edward, the fallen pastor.

Martha pitied many on that side of the shore, but she would not pity Edward. He had failed the test, cast out for turning away from God. He had chosen this depraved lifestyle. The others were ignorant, but Edward had known better. He was equipped with knowledge, better prepared for the Island than any of the others.

But he lacked conviction. God might forgive Edward one day, but Martha would not. Forgiveness was not her job.

Martha removed the hood of her burka and breathed in the clean air. Her face possessed a charismatic nobility with full, pale cheeks, serious brow, and lively, determined brown eyes. She dropped the hood to the sand and stared into the density of the Wilderness. The trees were as unyielding as the written Word, a mystery with no intention of being solved.

"Martha," a faceless follower said from beneath her veil.

Martha shut her eyes tightly, reaching for God.

Through the open door she had swung wide for Him, I slipped inside instead. She wouldn't notice the difference. No one ever did.

Within her soul, it was turbulent. Cold. Hot. Steady. Blustery. The emotions collided in violent fronts over plains stripped barren by winter. Tendrils of gray smoke climbed from the distance as wildfires raged. We stood side by side. She did not know me from God. She reached for my hand and I allowed her to take it. Her grip was tight, her fingers laced into mine with a territorial hunger.

"Martha," the follower implored, pulling us both out of Martha's mind. "I really gotta pee."

"Find a bush!"

The follower looked to the others. They shrugged. One pointed toward a clump of weeds just inside the woods.

"Gross," the follower squeaked.

Martha closed her eyes again. She stood once again before the roaring wildfires, angry, all-consuming, great pillars of flames all around her. She gazed into the fire, searched the heat for her God.

I stood behind her, unseen and unfelt. I wanted to comfort her as I always want to comfort humans. Her passion burned so intense that I hesitated. Even though it was an illusion, my fear was real.

"Help me," she said to the fire.

"Move on!" I said. "Do not fear the trees."

She spun toward me, seeing the God she knew of the Island. Black socks, flip flops, Hawaiian shirt, and an unreachable love.

I retreated from her mind, letting her imagination take full control again. Her eyes shot open, filled with tears. I was the sultry whisper of God. I used it at my own discretion, but whether inspiring the dictates of popes or guiding the will of dictators, I always spoke for Him. It lacked the glamour of flaming swords and skeletal, flying steeds, but that whisper had moved nations and altered history.

Martha's smile grew as her face flushed. She reached out for her hood. No one moved. She snapped her fingers and a follower snapped to, then snatched the hood from the sand and handed it to her.

"He wants us to find our home within the darkness," Martha announced, shaking the sand from the hood. "Job withstood the full force of Satan's treachery. We can withstand the Wilderness."

"How long?" a follower asked.

Martha slipped the hood over her head, struggled with the eyeholes, took the hood back off to reassess the position of the eyeholes, turned the hood around, put it back on, struggled more with the eyeholes. Finally, satisfied with her ability to see God's great Wilderness, she turned to face the others.

"Until ..." She trailed off as she adjusted the hood again so she could see better. "Until we have earned our place back in Heaven."

She motioned the followers onward toward the trees.

"Hold on, hold on," the follower pleaded from behind the clump of weeds. "I'm not done yet!"

Raul And His Lovely Guitar

"This could be fun," Todd whispered to Raul as they stood on the shore and watched the sprouted and curvy female exiles trudging through the waves. Todd had always had a thing for women and water, the way moisture smoothed and caressed the skin.

Raul offered Todd a conspiratorial smile, but his heart wasn't really in it. Sex was just a distant delicacy to Raul, a coping mechanism that had long ago lost its appeal. Raul never married, never fathered children. He simply kept women within his orbit. Or, rather, they kept him within theirs.

"You may not be boyfriend material," he'd heard a few too many times, "but I'm not going to let a fuck like you get away."

So women called when their other lovers fell through. They came to his door with broken and bitter hearts. Their bodies yearned for a surrogate, and Raul filled the role admirably. A career understudy. Attentive, curious, passionate with a voice that burned hot yet held back, like the ashes of an exhausted fire. He could read a woman within moments—their sexuality, their smiles, the way their eyes attacked or retreated, understanding who they were when the lights would go out, when they forgot their lives, their husbands, and their gods.

He overwhelmed them with quick, intense love affairs that came with an unspoken mutual understanding that someone would run. Women felt safe, knowing they could pack up and return home with no more luggage than what they'd brought with them.

As an old man he grew tired of the pattern, the ceremony of sex, the lightness of hope, the heaviness of inevitability. As he looked over the exiles, all beautiful in their own way, he already knew their quirks, needs, and shames.

He would become hungry again, he knew, but his new body was not energized as the others had been. He was not buzzing from new possibility, but instead felt weighed down by the emotional wreckage of old friends, dead lovers, and the fear of re-entering the dreary cycle of romance.

But he had his guitar. He had never written a song for a woman. He had certainly never played a song for a woman. He played only for his guitar, the body that willingly nestled into his arms whenever he called for her.

He considered all the guitars he'd ever owned as one continuation of a pure, undiminished romance. Unquestioned fidelity. A Fender was a Fender, a Godin was a Godin, a Les Paul was a Les Paul, but they were all one lover.

Raul's newest embodiment of that eternal love was the nameless dreadnought acoustic strapped to his back. It played cheap, like a Santa Cruz knock-off with worn strings and too much finish on its heavy, brittle wood. But it was no less his than that Gibson had been, the one he'd borrowed from Jackson Browne for a gig in Kansas City after his own equipment had been stolen. After watching the set, Browne told Raul to keep it. The guitar wanted to be in Raul's hands, Browne insisted. But Raul thanked Browne earnestly, handed the guitar over, and set out to find the next incarnation of his greatest love affair.

Todd nudged Raul and motioned further up the shoreline where Edward was hugging Ossie tightly, leaning his face into Ossie's shoulder to hide his tears. Billy and Sophia waited nearby, uncomfortable but needing information.

Closer to the woods, women talked nervously in a tight cluster as the men hovered on the periphery, everyone returning to the hormonal dystopia of early adulthood.

"Your girl's separated from the pack," Todd said. "Perfect time to strike."

Raul looked to the pianist, Edna, who stood alone, feet still in the water with her shoes in her hand. She was the only other musician Raul had met so far on the Island. When God cursed her with maturity, her brown hair had blossomed into a long, curled waterfall reaching to her lower back. Almost unfeasibly perfect hair, as if a magic salon fairy floated above her head, invisible and ever fretting about stray strands. A curious flourish for such an otherwise modest woman.

She met Raul's eyes and quickly looked away. Raul noticed her long and lean fingers. Perfect for a concert pianist.

"Go get her, boy," Todd said.

"Grow up."

Todd smiled. "I already did. And so did she and so did you. She's alone right now and I don't care if you go propose to her, tell her a fart joke, or give her a shoulder to cry on, but you are going even if I have to drag you."

Raul rolled his eyes. He took a breath, straightened his shirt and walked to Edna. She rewarded him with a weary half-smile. She was scared, he could tell. He slipped off his shoes and socks, leaving them at the shore as he walked through the water to reach her. They stood and let the small waves climb up and down their calves.

Raul leaned in.

"Let's find you a piano."

"They'd don't exactly grow on trees, do they?" she said. "Well, part of them does, I suppose."

"If I can swim back across the lake and steal you a piano, I will," Raul said.

Edna blushed and studied Raul. "Why?" she asked.

"Because playing music with you was the only time I have felt good since God stole me from Heaven."

She couldn't get the smile off her face. "Okay," she said. "Yes.

I'd love that. Thank you. But let's see what we can find on this side first, okay?"

"Okay."

I stood near the edge of the woods, waiting for the exiles to settle, waiting for the questions to come.

Martha the Believer
Part 2

When adolescent Martha thought of love, she imagined herself in the Badlands of South Dakota, bitter winds blowing through the buttes, her chest burst open, blood gushing out, her face flushed, her body desperate and ready to surrender.

When Martha sang in the choir, her voice strained to be let loose, to release all the passion walled up inside her.

So much love poured out of her.

With no receptacle to catch it.

"God is enough," she lied to herself as she tried to push fantasies of the preacher from her mind. When she turned seventeen, he transferred to a larger church in a larger town. The married preacher who replaced him didn't walk as righteous of a Christian path. This new man was heavier-set, bearded, and more charismatic. He snared Martha with stories of missionary work in South America.

The sex was surprising. Not good, not bad, just surprising. Her mother warned Martha that sex was painful and dangerous, but it wasn't either. It was just disappointing and awkward.

She left the church before anyone got wind of their affair. Next she found a ministry major who'd traveled to South Dakota for missionary work. The sex was a little better, mostly because he looked into her eyes most of the time. It was scary in a good way and they always talked a little afterwards.

She got pregnant. He retreated back to his Georgia bible college. She had a miscarriage. That was as close as Martha ever got to motherhood.

She dreamed of sex almost every night. Unable to starve her passion to death, she took to masturbation in hopes of bleeding it out, exhausting the temptation.

When she thought of sex, she thought of an incensed wolf snapping through the bars of a cage. The taste of it in her mind was bitter, but compelling; it brought her back.

"Where are we going, Martha?" a follower called as the five women trudged through the Wilderness, crossing trails and pushing onward.

Martha paused. She considered offering words of encouragement, perhaps scripture, but nothing came to mind. She had no answers, couldn't think of inspiring quotations, she only knew to continue moving forward until God spoke to her. She bent a branch out of the way and stepped over a tangle of weeds.

The hum of an approaching airplane brought Martha's eyes up through the forest canopy to a small halo of sky. A low-flying plane roared overhead toward the runway outside the campground on the other side of the lake.

"Please," Martha prayed silently, but to no answer.

Martha opened her eyes, adjusted her hood, then started.

A young black couple stood only a few feet away, stunned as they studied the group of white-sheeted women. The man stepped in front of the woman, his stance wide, his fists clenched.

Martha noticed the couple was wearing new clothes—cargo pants and jungle boots, him a plain black t-shirt, her a sleeveless top. These were not clothes from the campground.

Martha opened her mouth to speak. Closed it. Opened it again and managed "Hello." It was muffled by her hood.

"Hi," the man replied, hesitant.

"I love your boots," a follower added diplomatically.

"Thank you," the woman said.

"We need your help!" another follower called from behind Martha.

Martha shot up a hand to silence her. The couple said nothing.

"We are new to this side of the Island and could use a meal, perhaps a little guidance," Martha said.

"Uh huh," the woman said.

"I assure you, we mean no harm," Martha said. "We are children of God."

"Oh my!" another follower chirped, looking down at her white sheet, then up to the couple. "We aren't the KKK, if that's what you are thinking!"

Martha glanced at her own sheet. Her face flushed warm and red.

"We are merely trying to be humble before the eyes of God!" Martha insisted, awkwardly.

"Uh huh," the woman repeated.

"We only wear white because that was all that we had," a third follower offered. "Would it help if we wore a different color?"

The man motioned for the woman to continue on the trail leading away from the group.

"You'll find food that way," the man said, pointing in the opposite direction.

"God bless you, sir," Martha said, holding up her hands, palms together, bowing slightly.

The man frowned, then turned to follow the woman. Just before disappearing into the trees, he paused and glanced back at the group.

"And yes, any color but white would be helpful."

Raul And His Lovely Guitar
Part 2

One of four. That's what she told Raul—he was part of a quartet all sharing her as a single instrument. Together they would become her perfect man.

Raul was the lover, the one to worship her, the one who knew her body, the one who knew her heart. He called her the "white buffalo," looking upon her in reverence and awe, the same way believers gazed upon the Notre Dame. She was an impossibility. A lone, rare jewel that he wanted all to his own. But she wouldn't allow it.

He wept when he finally severed his life from hers. He could not touch his guitar for weeks. He was afraid of the music that would pour out.

She was gone now—along with all the women he had adored, the venues he had haunted, the musicians he had understood, the records he had scratched out with the sounds he'd devoted a life to studying.

When he looked over to the other exiles crowding around me as I spoke about the Wilderness, he pulled the guitar to his chest and held it like a frightened mother.

"And you will find life easier to manage," I told the exiles. "Your choices are your own. I will show you to food and fresh water, the farmers among you will find the soil is rich and yielding. The Wilderness has made some very happy, but it has driven others mad. Stay with your group. Do not travel alone. Find your place in this world and look out for one another."

"Where is Tommy?" Edward asked.

The exiles glanced up in surprise. Only those in Edward's inner circle—Billy, Sophia, and Ossie—knew the boy with the beautiful ocean eyes had survived the fall from the Island and was now living somewhere in the Wilderness.

"He is roaming," I said. "I can't say where exactly. Somewhere in the Wilderness, deep within its heart. I suggest letting him find his own way back home."

"And the others?" Billy asked.

"They are all alive." I raised my hand and pointed toward the Wilderness. "The sun sets in the west behind the Wilderness—" I turned to point toward the campground across the lake. "And it rises in the East." I pointed toward the corner of the Island. "Petrov lives alone somewhere on the southwest edge."

"Barry and Mary are living happily together," I said, dropping my hands. "Privacy is important to them and they prefer to remain hidden in the Wilderness, but I will let them know you've arrived. I imagine you will see them when it is time."

"And Simon?" Todd asked.

"I don't know," I said with an amused shrug. "I know that he's alive, but he wants to remain hidden. He is—he is making the most of his time on the Island, just as I hope that you do. This is an opportunity. God is not abandoning you. He is devoted to all of you. His plan may never make sense to us, but He will take you back to Paradise."

"When?" Sophia asked, her arms crossed tightly over her chest, the fingers of her right hand laced with Billy's which was draped over her shoulder.

"When it's time. I'm sorry; I can't tell you more than that."

"How many of us have there been?" Billy asked. "How many groups came before us?"

"Twenty-three," I answered. "There are currently 483 souls on the Island."

A hum brought the group's eyes to the sky. The sound grew louder until God's plane appeared, skimming over Heaven. It passed overhead. I closed my eyes. I leapt from my body into the cockpit of the plane, finding the mind of an angel. Then I jumped from one human mind to another and another, recounting their past lives and mourning their rebirths.

"488," I corrected myself. "Soon there will be 512."

"And we can die in the Wilderness?" Billy asked. "What happens after that? Do we go to Heaven?"

"I don't know," I lied. The truth wouldn't do them any good. "Just stay safe, keep your friends close, and wait for the end."

I attempted an encouraging smile as I met their eyes. Some were dubious, some were angry, but all were sad and afraid.

"Come, let me show you around," I said, turning from the lake to the trees. I paused, had a brief argument with myself on my role as their surrogate father. I faced the group.

"Um, I don't want to make it weird, but since you are adults and the birds and the bees are a thing now ..." I trailed off as brief and uncomfortable laughter spread through the group. "Women can't get pregnant, so, have fun with that—I guess."

I shrugged and walked to the trees.

"Who else is out there?" Billy called as the group followed me towards a small path. "Who do we need to be worried about?"

"As I said, the Wilderness is growing darker by the day. There are no good guys or bad guys. It is more complicated than that. But I can say this: stay out of the center of the Wilderness. Everything you need is along the shore and the edges. Don't go into the heart."

"Isn't that where Tommy is?" Edward asked.

I glanced back at Edward.

"Yes. He's traveled into the darkest corner of that heart. That's why he doesn't want you going after him."

Martha the Believer
Part 3

Dementia came for Martha's mother. It swept in with the fall winds, the crumbling woman's memories dropping away like the fragile autumn leaves. By the first snow, her mother's mind was gone. She snuggled into a warm insanity to wait out the brutal South Dakota winter.

Martha was only twenty-four when she died. She remembered waking to a butcher knife embedded in her chest. She remembered her mother stroking Martha's hair with her bloody fingers. She remembered her mother cooing "This Little Light of Mine". Her mother was a lovely singer, even with a hollowed out mind.

Martha died with only a vague awareness of having been murdered. Her body would be discovered three weeks later after her mother was found dead beside a country road a half mile from the house, her corpse preserved by a snowdrift.

As Martha felt the tug of Heaven, a great release came over her spirit. Her love, dammed up for so long, now flowed without fear or shame. Martha sensed other spirits, felt embraced, an orgasmic joy that never ebbed, never gave way to alienation or abandonment. His glory now eclipsed the pain that had once twisted and darkened her thoughts.

She reveled in the embrace of a million lovers, unencumbered by thoughts of self or any trace of regret. She felt only love and the overwhelming proximity of Him.

Since she arrived to the Island, Martha had been fighting back feelings of resentment that followed her eviction from Paradise. It was a battle she waged with every breath and every heartbeat.

Hold onto your faith. No matter the tribulations, hold onto

your faith.

Though Martha was lost in the Wilderness, she was certain destiny would present itself. She heard God's encouraging voice pressing her on. She imagined His touch. Electric and certain.

That was my voice in her head, of course. I'd always been good at plagiarizing the Old Man.

"So, if we can't call them 'black' or 'colored', what are we supposed to call them now?" one follower asked another, evidence of the thirty-five year gap between their lives on Earth.

"African American," the second follower declared. "That was the new thing. I think we voted on it or something."

"That's stupid," a third follower jumped in. "First, we never voted on calling anyone anything. Second, they ain't African. Not no more. We all just from the Island. We're Islanders."

The third follower sounded particularly proud of this revelation, as if she'd waited months to introduce the phrase, certain it would take hold if she just waited for the right moment.

"You make us sound like fat Polynesians," Martha said.

Apparently, that moment had not yet arrived

"Polynesians aren't all fat," the third follower countered, speaking more timidly than before. "Hula girls are real pretty."

"Yeah, and they got some hunky football players," someone else added. "I don't mind a man carrying a little extra weight as long as he carries it right."

Martha motioned for the group to stop.

"Shut up so I can think," Martha said. She peered down the winding path that soon disappeared into dense vegetation that hid whatever oasis the black man had insisted lay ahead.

Martha ripped the hood from her head and gulped in the fresh, cool air. She closed her eyes and listened hard, but there was only silence.

"What am I doing wrong, Lord?" Martha whispered. She

looked down at the hood, clutched in her hands. It'd once been a pillowcase. She let it drop to the ground.

"Look, y'all!" a follower chirped. "It's Bambi!"

A fawn peered at them through the trees, its eyes so large and black they almost seemed impossible. Its ears flicked away gnats that buzzed around its head.

"She's so cute, ohmygawd!" one follower cooed.

"Should we kill it for food?" a second follower asked.

No one objected.

"A sign," Martha murmured. She felt the clammy skin on her face. She felt her own smile forming. She turned to the others. "It's a sign. We are blind with our hoods."

"But it is unseemly to allow men to see our faces," a follower said in a practiced tone. "They'll molest us with their eyes. That's what you said."

"Only God can deem what is decent and what is vile," Martha announced, louder than necessary. "Now remove your bonds and greet His gift with virgin eyes!"

The followers timidly removed their hoods, revealing flushed faces and mussed hair.

"His gift smells like poop," Melinda whispered only to be shushed by Cheyenne.

Willow was the last to remove her hood, revealing sculpted cheekbones, smooth, tanned skin and rich green eyes. She possessed the kind of face that started wars and wrecked marriages. She was also the tallest of the group, which was not lost on anyone but Willow. It was the first time any of the followers had seen her without her hood since they'd grown into adults.

Willow reached to her face. "Somethin' wrong?"

They studied her and scowled.

"Yeah," Martha began. "I think you might have a rash or

something. It looks weird, maybe you should keep your hood on."

"Ya think? Am I gonna be okay?"

"Yeah," Cheyenne said. "But you'll wanna keep the rash out of the sunlight."

"And we don't want it to spread," April added.

"Oh, alright, then," Willow whimpered, slipping the hood back on.

Cheyenne and April traded smirks.

The women turned as the fawn began walking along the path.

"Onward!" Martha proclaimed, motioning them forward.

"So, we are or are not gonna eat Bambi?" Willow asked. Martha refused to answer partly because she didn't know, but mostly because Willow was now her least favorite of the group.

***

They came upon a small group of unoccupied huts, all only about seven feet tall, with slanted roofs made of branches. They were the kind of primitive structures Martha had seen in a National Geographic magazine once during a visit to the county free clinic.

"I wonder if there's a bathroom somewhere," Willow asked.

"Are you kidding?" Cheyenne shot back. "How is it physically possible for you to need to pee again?"

"I don't need to pee," Willow said. "I need to do the other thing."

The group ignored Willow and pushed along the path. Whoever built the shanties had abandoned them long ago, but there were no signs of violence. It looked as if they'd simply left.

The fawn walked slowly along the trail, looking back from time to time to verify the women were still following. The path opened up into a wide clearing. The group stopped at the end of the trail and gazed up to a camouflage canopy spread across the sky, similar to what militaries used to hide artillery. It hung twenty feet from the ground, tied to trees encircling the clearing.

The clearing was empty aside from a post sticking up from the ground with a mass of mutilated meat impaled on it. It appeared to Martha to have been a partially cooked hog with its legs torn off and remaining flesh picked at by scavengers.

Beside the post was a mudpit that measured about fifteen feet across. The fawn didn't seem at all bothered by the carcass and strode out to the mudpit where it turned and waited for the group.

Martha scanned the clearing, but saw no movement.

"Who's hungry?" Martha asked, walking toward the post.

"I don't eat meat," Willow said. No one responded, so she added, "it's cruel." Still no takers, so she followed.

As Martha approached, her mouth salivated at the rich, fatty smell of the seared meat. It resembled a pig she'd once seen cooked over a fire on a spit at a summer church luau.

A human head jerked up from the torso. Willow screamed and the others bolted away. The carcass's head turned to the scattered group. Burnt skin flaked off its torn face, its eyes were blood red, and only small patches of hair survived on the scarred, bloody scalp.

"Hello," the head called. Only by the voice did Martha recognize it as a man. She heard no pain in the voice, but an eerie calm. "Don't be shy, come on."

Martha spread out her hands, gathering her followers behind her.

"What is this witchery?" Martha called, really liking how the phrasing shot out of her mouth.

"This is the Wilderness, child," the head responded. "We are all witches here."

The followers looked to Martha. She was surprised and stymied by his brazen blasphemy. She then wondered if "blasphemy" was even the right word. It wasn't, she decided but couldn't decide on a better alternative.

"Martha," Cheyenne whispered.

"We are not witches," Martha proclaimed. "We are children of God!"

"To survive, you will have to be both."

The fawn turned from the body and dipped its head to the surface of the mudpit. The women watched in disgust as it slurped up the mud as if it was fresh water.

"Come, eat," the head called, looking down to the mudpit.

"Are you kidding?" Cheyenne asked.

"This is the life source of the Island," the head replied. "All that food in the campground? It came from the mudpits. Pure nutrients. There is no need to farm, no need to hunt. The Island provides."

Martha motioned for the group to follow her to the mudpit. The fawn lifted its head, shook the mud from its snout, and moved out of the group's way.

"We are in a new Eden," the head said. "A terrible, lonely, and vicious Eden where we know truth but cannot be expelled."

The analogy didn't sound right to Martha, but she'd never been good at arguing theology. The idea of God had always seemed contradictory, in Martha's mind, to that of reason. She remained silent as she knelt before the mudpit and dipped her hand into the mud. Small bubbles rose to the surface. The mud felt warm and thick. She lifted her hand to her lips and drank. She rolled the warm, syrupy broth in her mouth, coating her palate. It was rich, somewhat creamy, but mostly dense like a beef stew that had been pureed.

It was pleasant. She'd eaten much worse while growing up

poor on government handouts. Martha remembered a time when her mother boiled dry dog food. The mudpit was at least better than that.

She motioned to the others. They hesitated, so Martha snapped and pointed to the mudpit. One by one, they approached, knelt, and drank. Only small sips, only as an act of contrition. Willow was careful with her hood, lifting it only enough to bring the broth to her mouth. After Cheyenne's first sip, she began drinking in slurps.

"Look at me all you want," Cheyenne huffed. "I think it's good."

"What's your name?" Willow asked the mangled man.

"Trevor. Yours?"

"Willow. What happened to you?"

"What happened to you?" the man shot back.

Willow reached up to touch her hood.

"I have a skin condition," Willow admitted.

"We don't want it to spread," April said.

Trevor studied Willow, then April, passing judgment.

"Does it hurt?" Willow asked.

"Not anymore."

"Do you want us to take you off there?" Willow asked, stepping closer to Trevor.

"The men who placed me here will want me to stay here," he said. "I appreciate the offer, but I could not bear the thought of you suffering because you wanted to help."

Willow fell instantly in love. It was her way.

"Who are they?" Martha asked, standing up and approaching the man.

"Islanders, like us?" Willow asked, trying out the name again.

"Islanders? I like that," Trevor said. Willow blushed beneath the hood. "I suppose they are Islanders, but not like you or me. You will know them when they decide to find you. You will know they are the ones trying to take control of the Island."

"God is in control of the Island," Martha proclaimed.

"Only if we let Him, my dear."

I Cannot Die
Part 3

I am ashamed at how the business with Job got away from me. My relationship with God is complicated and bitter, as you would imagine, but I never enjoyed making humans suffer. Certainly not like what happened with that poor man.

The Bible stated that we were testing Job, measuring the endurance of his faith, but that is not true. I never doubted Job would cling to the love of his Creator. He was human, after all. When adversity, fear, and horror rain down, humans turn to gods and art and love and infinite abstractions. They take comfort from the silence, the hope for something eternal that will sweep them up from the misery.

You don't destroy a man's faith through torture. You destroy it with abundance.

If I had truly wanted to test Job, I would have fertilized his fields, inspired a fierce seductive spirit in his bedroom, and encouraged productivity among his children and his workers. Let luxury do the damage.

I didn't want to test the man. I wanted to test his Creator. God had spoken of His deep love for His chosen people, so I was curious to see how much injustice He would let them endure simply to protect His pride.

Quite a lot, apparently. It was my fault that it got out of hand. I should have known better. After Job, I decided to change the way I did business. I would feed mankind's needs and desires, picking off God's favored believers by aiding them in building a glorious, global civilization. Heaven on Earth, so they would no longer needed prayer, religion, or servitude to a voyeur gleefully watching as wars and famine inspired worship and devotion.

But Earth was a lost cause. It was hurtling toward the Rapture and would continue on its way, despite my best efforts. God had a clear plan for the Earth that was inescapable. As far as I knew, the Wilderness lacked the same divine destiny. The perpetual hand of God no longer pressed down on man as it did on Earth. I saw the Wilderness as an opportunity to see how humanity could grow without God's stunting mysticism.

I was astonished with the miracles I witnessed on the Island, even within the scope of my long and well-traveled life. I'd witnessed angels war in the ether, suns conceived from celestial dust. I was the lone creation to step freely between Heaven and Hell.

I was damned, but I was not truly imprisoned. God still needed me as an errand boy to run back and forth to the one place He refused to go.

Then came the day He personally retrieved me, offering a pardon if I helped Him with a new Creation. An experiment, really, and we would work together again.

I had hoped we might accomplish something significant on the Island.

I was a fool to trust Him.

Now, billions of miles away from Earth and the Island, I watch stars dying, the fabric of the cosmos stretching ever thinner, ever weaker. I find myself hurtling toward the Wall. I am falling from His center, outpacing the expansion of the stars, racing toward the end of all we have ever known.

It gives me hope, it truly does. Once I pass through the Wall, I will know either death or life. I will no longer exist in between.

I want to tell my story for as long as I can. I want to tell you how the Island changed the course of His universe. I hope I can continue sending my story back to you once I have crossed over for good, to let you know what lies beyond God's Love.

Petrov the Painter

Love destroys. Its vast, all-consuming fire produces a heat that cannot be suffocated, but burns and burns until there is nothing left but a sorrowful sky above fields of smoldering ash.

Then comes the cold. The terrible cold.

Petrov's hand searched under the silk blankets and found Julia's naked hip. She slid toward him, pressed her back to his chest and turned her face to allow him a kiss. Then she rolled away to continue sleeping while Petrov rose and sat on the edge of the bed. He looking up at Desya's unfinished eyes. The twelve-foot mosaic of his dead wife loomed over the bedroom. It was surrounded by bookcases filled with old and worn works of literature, philosophy, history, and criticism. Sketches of faces and still life covered the walls while paint splatters dotted the concrete floor. A large, oak wardrobe stood in the corner. Solar tubes embedded in the bunker's ceilings cast sunlight throughout the bunker. Petrov had electric lamps and work lights, too, but he only used them at night. The power grid was fed by solar-powered batteries, and they required all day to recharge.

I detest aggrandizement, but this was a time when the term "move Heaven and Earth" might actually have applied. So many of us had pitched into building the Island's lone artist a temple. We did it because we had lost a god. We had to find another creator to worship.

Another creator to fight over.

Petrov slid his feet into pale blue slippers, walked to his wardrobe, and pulled out a white robe. The bunker was chilly, but it was safe. That was a luxury few in the Wilderness could enjoy. Petrov was more celebrated and rewarded for his art on the Island than he'd ever been on Earth.

He walked to the mosaic and gently ran his fingers over the

small slivers of tiles, tracing the lines of Desya's hand, almost feeling her fingers reaching for his. Some women forced Petrov to tack a blanket over the mosaic, but Julia did not. She never even mentioned it. Maybe out of respect, but probably out of stubbornness.

Petrov loved Julia. He slept with her as often as the difficult girl made herself available. She spent her time combing the Island for knowledge, for the answers to make sense of its place in the universe and her place on the Island. A lifelong atheist, she'd been dismayed when she awoke on the plane ride above Heaven to find out that she'd been wrong all along. As far as Petrov knew, she was the only atheist chosen for the Island.

"Did He bring you up from Hell?" Petrov once asked her.

"He brought me up from darkness," Julia answered in her careful, earnest tone. Being correct was important to her and she often picked her words as methodically as an old lady digging through an apple crate. "But I wouldn't call it 'Hell'. I was not unhappy there. In fact, I had never felt so free. That said, I wouldn't call it pleasant, either."

Petrov's love for Julia was different than his love for Desya, who had given her whole self, without reservation. To love Julia was to grasp for mist. She simply could not be had. She did not want to be had, and she wouldn't allow herself to be had. Petrov wanted her all the more.

But she was just one of many women Petrov loved. Each of them devastated him in her own way, keeping Petrov in a perpetual cycle of angst and joy.

Love is fire.
Fire is energy.
Energy creates art.
Art is happiness.

Happiness is love.

Julia would leave today and Petrov would mourn. He knew the pattern well, but he also knew another woman would soon take her place. Many lovers rotated through Petrov's bed, lured by the novelty of a painter in a land bereft of art. Desya would not have approved of Petrov's lifestyle. For her, it was one woman to every man. Desya had been disturbed by American culture, by how freely women gave themselves. And by how their eldest daughter, Mayla, had embraced that lifestyle.

Mayla. The beautiful Mayla.

And Natalia, their other daughter. So smart. So serious. So much like Desya. Pretty, like Desya, but not as bold as Mayla.

They had all died in the Rapture.

Petrov's soul chilled as he thought of Templetown. The community was gone now, along with all who had lived within it. He shook the memories away, or rather unsettled them so they would drift back into the recesses of his mind. Their ghosts would emerge again, as they did every night in his dreams once the fog of alcohol cleared.

Petrov turned to Julia. She was awake now, her stern blue eyes on Petrov, a blanket pulled up modestly over her chest. She allowed a cocky smile.

"Morning, darling," she said. "Go cook me something."

"Yes, my love."

Petrov grabbed another robe from the wardrobe and tossed it onto the bed.

***

An imposing icebox dominated Petrov's kitchen. A gift from me. The Engineers delivered ice once a week and groceries twice a week. Petrov had asked for none of these things; they were freely given by the Engineers "for services rendered and yet to be rendered." The Engineers also provided many of his painting supplies. Petrov did not know where they found them, nor did he care.

There had been a time when only the angels and I could bring back the relics of Earth, but The Engineers were getting stronger and more creative every day. They were starting to see the many holes within space and time.

The bunker had been dug out by the Americans, who used mud from the pits to fashion the walls. The Americans were building a new society which would need art, symbology, and all the other things a nation must possess to prove its greatness. Many Americans lived in shanties hidden within the trees, but New Wichita was experimenting with underground dwellings. If they could not build their empires up, as they had on Earth, they would build them down instead.

Petrov was disturbed by the lavish presents bestowed upon him. Just as he was disturbed by the Island and what he'd seen the Americans and the Engineers do. Their generosity provided him with the freedom to create art. He knew accepting their gifts was wrong, but Petrov was on the Island to create. God told him this. Petrov was not an expert in politics, in governance, or in religion. He knew how to create art, so that is what he would do, in God's name.

That miserable bastard.

The eggs were a true delicacy, and probably drew more visitors to Petrov's bunker than his art or his skill in the bedroom. These were not the artificial eggs Petrov had eaten in the campground, which had been nothing but lard disguised as eggs. These were real eggs from real chickens. Only the Americans had them, and they supplied Petrov with two dozen every week. The fruits and the vegetables were rare as well, but more of the exiles were learning how to cultivate crops within the forest, hidden from the sky by thin, camouflage canopies.

There were even larger livestock starting to emerge. From where, none of the exiles really knew. It seemed to Petrov as if there were two gods of the Island. One who created new life and one who squashed it when it encroached on the campground. It added to the mystery and the possibility of the Wilderness. Ill-defined laws of reality made for a belief that all things might actually be possible, yet it could all be undone in a moment if God fell into a mood. There was nothing more freeing to humans than fatalism.

Petrov rarely indulged in the lard from the mudpits, aside from the bacon made by the Americans. This was not the overly-crisp fare from the campground, but rather a thin, delicate, moist bacon that cooked perfectly and dripped with a maple note, especially when fried with a little natural butter. The bacon was from the mudpit to the northeast of New Wichita.

The gas stove was another great luxury. It was a gift from me. I trusted him with the stove because I knew he was not the type to look for the answer. It worked and that was enough for him.

The scent of spattering bacon finally stirred Julia from the bed. She padded through the kitchen, past Petrov, and toward the dining room to await her meal. She wore a purple, green, and dark blue gypsy skirt with a tight black shirt—sleeveless, to show off her delicate shoulders—and an olive gray Legionnaire jacket.

Three metallic bangs echoed through the bunker. Petrov put down his spatula and looked to Julia as her face paled. She'd been here once before when the Americans arrived, and Petrov had thought she would never come back. Petrov met her eyes, saw the horror. There was nothing he could do for her. Julia knew this was the compromise of living under Petrov's roof.

Julia stood and marched back to the bedroom. "I fucking hate this island!"

He knew she would leave without breakfast. Perhaps this time it would be for good.

Petrov turned off the burner and tightened his robe. He wound through the bunker to the stairs that led to the blast door. He climbed to the top, then leaned against the metal door and peered through a peephole. He saw only forest.

Petrov sighed and spun the handle until the lock disengaged. Sunlight poured in as the heavy door swept open to reveal, side by side at the doorstep, three severed heads.

Their eyes were open, alive, and terrified.

Ossie the Widower

Ossie was capable of killing a man. He did not fight often while on Earth since his size often prevented him from becoming a target, but he'd fought enough to know that it was something he did well. Two men in New Orleans came to mind. A Mexican with a candy skull tattooed on his neck and a bald white guy wearing an Affliction t-shirt under a satin blazer. Ossie was defending Isaac, who was drunk, obnoxious, and overly free that night. Ossie didn't remember much aside from Isaac screaming for Ossie to stop, the blood soaking into Ossie's new shoes, his knuckles breaking against the Mexican's skull. Isaac pulled Ossie off the man and out the back door into an alley of the French Quarter, leaving the two battered young assailants to bleed out.

As the group wound through the Wilderness, dread walked with Ossie, just as it had in New Orleans, in Chicago, in Mississippi, in Manchester, in Jamaica. Ossie rarely felt light, even as a child. He was always aware of the thousands of eyes always watching and waiting. Shopkeepers, nervous parents, drunken skinheads, policemen. He preferred the tension; he was familiar with it. Danger was a difficult but reliable friend. When he decided that he would kill for his fellow exiles, it was a commitment of love.

"Live your life."

Isaac had been in the hospital bed for weeks by that point, the machines pinging in the periphery, the smell of bleach and chemicals permeating everything, death on the near horizon.

"Live your life."

But how? Ossie hadn't made a major life decision without Isaac's consultation for three decades. Never made a step without Isaac's fingers laced in his. When Isaac died, Ossie followed within months because—why stay?

"Live your life."

What does that mean, here, on the Island? Find a gay boy and carve out a place on the shore? Take up writing again? Try to love? There was no life that Ossie could see. There was simply survival.

Well, there was Edward. That poor lost soul. And there were Ossie's friends.

But no Isaac, his North Star. Theirs had not been a perfect love, but it had been love, and the stability of family that stayed. Ossie's mother and his sisters had learned to love Ossie for who he really was, but it took time. Isaac had loved him from the moment they met. It was at the Pilsen East Artists' Open house. Isaac called Ossie out for name-dropping. A teasing argument ensued. Somehow Isaac ended up on the roof of the apartment complex, weeping softly as he confessed everything he'd ever done wrong while Ossie held him. All his sins were small and silly; it had taken Buddha-like control to stifle laughter at the more embarrassing moments. But they were important to Isaac, so they became important to Ossie.

They never spent more than two days apart from that moment on.

Even after so much time, alone on the Island, Ossie felt a phantom tingle in his chest where Isaac should be. They both died Christians, so Isaac was swimming somewhere in Heaven. One small thread among millions. Ossie remembered gliding through Heaven with Isaac by his side, or at least with the impression that Isaac was always close. He could not know for sure, but Isaac had felt immediate from the first moment of Ossie's ascension until his rebirth on the plane as it soared toward the Island.

Ossie's thoughts so enveloped him that he didn't notice the pit until his right foot sank into the warm mud. He flailed his arms to maintain balance. Billy grabbed Ossie's shirt and yanked him back. Ossie jerked his leg out. The pit exhaled a sucking sound as it relinquished his foot but kept his shoe as a trophy.

Laughter came and Ossie shook his head, laughing himself. He glanced around at a small clearing in the forest, where a bit of sky broke through the canopy of trees. Ossie sighed and knelt down to dig through the slop for his shoe.

"So, try not to walk through the pits," I began. "Since this is your primary food source."

The amusement ebbed as the exiles tried to decide if I was serious.

"Some pits are marked," I continued. "You will know the markings when you see them, but this pit is neutral. No one owns it, so feel free to make camp nearby. The pits are not particularly appetizing, I grant you, but they are safe and filled with all the nutrients you will ever need. You are free to fish at night. You can grow fruits and vegetables, provided you can cover your crops so they can't be seen from the sky. You can even hunt, but you do not need to in order to survive."

I knelt down to the pit. I scooped up a handful of the mud and held it up.

"Contaminants cannot survive in the pits," I said. "Even if someone attempted to poison the pits, it would not affect you. This is God's gift to you, His promise that, whatever else the Island lacks, you will never have to go hungry."

I took a bite of the mud. To me, it tasted like bland Nutella. Rich, creamy, faintly sweet, but overwhelmed by a buttery, savory heaviness. It didn't possess a very strong smell, but there was a roasted acorn note. Every pit possessed its own character, its own taste. Some of the pits further toward the center of the Island were heavy, meaty, almost a stew, which is why the Americans coveted them. Toward the western edge, the pits were thinner, lighter, less expressive.

What can I say? I am a connoisseur. It's what makes me good at my job.

I held the mud out to Billy. He shrugged and swiped a fingerful and stuck it in his mouth. He moved the mud around his palate, then swallowed heavily.

"I guess it'll do," Billy said, his voice devoid of enthusiasm.

"There is a barter system in place within the Wilderness," I said, tossing the rest of the mud to the ground, then wiping my hand off on my shorts. "If you can create something of value, then you can trade for real food. Just be very cautious when dealing with other groups. Some of them are very willing to take advantage of new exiles."

I heard the pit burp and looked over to see Ossie had retrieved his shoe. He stamped the mud off the shoe then used grass to clean it off the best he could.

"The water from the lake will always be drinkable," I said. "There are springs throughout the Island. Explore, find your place, but be careful."

"Of who?" Billy asked.

"Everyone, at first," I said. "Choose your friends carefully."

A thread of warmth wound through my mind. A call. I closed my eyes to listen.

"Bali?" Sophia asked.

I opened my eyes. "I'm needed in the campground."

"Bringing in more children?" Edward asked.

"Yes. It can't all fall on Jay to be the shepherd."

"How do we contact you if we need something?" Todd asked.

"When you truly need me, I will find you. I am not your keeper; I am not a babysitter. I won't often intervene in the Wilderness. Do not count on me, and do not count on God. On the Island, you create your own miracles."

I was pretty pleased with my closing line. An introduction to the Wilderness rarely went that smoothly. I patted Billy on the shoulder and walked through the group of exiles, back toward the shore, glad they'd been too shocked to ask more questions.

***

After minutes passed with only racing minds, Billy began directing groups to comb the immediate area for places to set camp.

"Stay close," he added. "We have no idea who is out there."

From the trees, shadowed figures watched.

Petrov the Painter
Part 2

Petrov removed the heads from his doorstep so Julia could leave. She would not return. The reality of loving a man like Petrov was simply too much, as it had been for every other woman who had stepped through that hatch and on towards his bed.

Petrov retrieved pillows from his workspace for each of the severed heads. One at a time, he cradled them gently, walking them to his ventilated workspace on the other end of the bunker. It was a small room, dark except for a single skylight that beamed down onto his workbench. A metal drum was tucked away in the corner. A fan in the ceiling creaked as it funneled air out of the room and up to the surface of the Island. Shelves on the walls were draped with shadows.

Though alive, the severed heads could not talk. They could only gaze with tired, sad eyes. Petrov would never find out why the heads had come to his doorstep. He knew who had brought them, and that was enough.

Petrov returned for Julia and escorted her safely to the blast door. She fled with a conflicted smile. She felt a great sympathy for the poor, trapped artist, but this was not her life. It could not be her life.

Petrov was well practiced in the art of hiding beneath the atrocities, surviving, remaining quiet, waiting it out. He was not a revolutionary; he was not an activist. He was an artist. He only wanted to create. He left the destroying to everyone else.

He surveyed the heads. Two men. One woman. Even with her face a grim purple and the skin of her neck shredded grotesquely, Petrov saw in the woman's youthful cheeks and expressive blue eyes the soft beauty of a romantic intellectual. Her pensive, pale lips tried for words she had no breath to form.

His heart tumbled in his chest, the agony driving him to love her deeply. He loved all these poor souls that were condemned to his lab.

Love is fire.
Fire is energy.
Energy creates art.
Art is agony.
Agony is love.

He placed the woman's head next to the others on the workbench, all facing Petrov as he pulled a chair close to them. He sat and studied their curious and tragic faces.

"You may already know me," Petrov began. "I am an artist. I am very sorry that you are here."

He met their eyes, one at a time.

"I do not believe that any of us have ever met," Petrov continued. "I do not know why you were brought to me. I do not care to know what you have done to upset the Americans. I only wish to serve you in these final moments of your life."

The female head managed a single tear, her lips trembling and twisted in sorrow.

"One blink equals 'yes;' two blinks equals 'no'. Do you understand?"

They blinked once.

"Are you in pain?"

The two men blinked "no," but the woman blinked "yes."

Petrov nodded. He knelt to reach for a toolbox sitting beside the workbench. It scraped against the concrete floor as he slid it closer. The heads' eyes followed Petrov's every movement as he opened the toolbox, retrieved a plastic bottle with no label, and set it on the workbench.

Then he stood and walked into the shadows. A metal latched clattered and an old cabinet squeaked. Petrov returned with a clean, white towel. He opened the plastic bottle and poured a clear liquid on the towel, then laid the towel flat on the workbench.

"With your permission?" Petrov asked as he reached for the woman. She blinked "yes."

He lifted the head from its pillow, then placed it on the towel. Its eyes fluttered, then closed. The tense facial muscles slackened. The eyes opened again, glassy but still lucid. She smiled, then mouthed a "thank you".

After carefully balancing the head back on its pillow, Petrov removed the towel and tossed it into a trash can on the other end of his workbench. He sat down and looked to each head carefully as he spoke.

"I can end this, if you want me to. I will only take your lives with your permission. I do not know what happens after death. I do not know if you return to Heaven. I can make you no promises aside from an end to this suffering. If you decide to die, you will be placed in acid which will quickly clean off all the flesh and matter, leaving only bone. It is the only way to assure death, to sever the soul from your body."

Then Petrov stood and walked back into the shadows.

"This is the job that has been given to me," Petrov called from the darkness. "If you have not heard my name, you have certainly seen my work before."

Petrov returned from the shadows, a skull in his hand. A purple and black war mask had been painted on it. "Beware" was scrawled in a angry lettering along both sides of the skull. Petrov had devoted hundreds of hours of small line work, following the contours of the skull. The design emerged on this skull as an individual expression as unique as the mind that it once encased. He was very proud. He had known the man to whom it had once belonged. A kind man who was the first person Petrov had met in the Wilderness and, as it turned out, the man who had saved Petrov's life.

The Americans had let Petrov keep the skull for this moment. To show the condemned their ultimate fate.

The heads stared at the skull. The woman looked as if she was trying to cry, but she had no more moisture for tears.

As Petrov turned the skull in the beam of sunlight, he felt a mix of shame and pride. He returned the skull to its shadowed resting place. At the cabinet, he lingered for a moment and pressed his forehead against the skull's. He wanted to pray, but to whom?

Then he returned to the bench and sat. "If you would like to live, I will respect your wishes," he said. "But I warn you, your lives will become more miserable. Your brains know that you are depleted, that you cannot drink, breathe, or eat. This pain will consume you. All those before you who tried to live ultimately chose to die. On Earth, I witnessed the violent murders of my wife and daughters, but even that is not as horrible as watching one of you suffer starvation."

Petrov took a moment. He looked away from the heads down to his trembling hands folded on the table.

"I cannot tell you how sorry I feel for you," Petrov said, eyes still down, voice barely louder than a whisper. "I cannot tell you how ashamed I am to be the last man you will ever see. But someone must be."

Petrov stood and walked across the room. He rifled through the shelves as the heads looked to each other. Petrov opened a drawer and returned to the workbench as he pulled on protective gloves that looked like cooking mitts that covered his forearms.

"Do you want to live?"

It took the heads time to process the question, but the two men eventually blinked "no."

The woman looked up to the poor, tortured artist, studying his sorrowful eyes. He was alone, she decided, and she wouldn't abandon him. Not yet.

She blinked "yes."

Ossie the Widower
Part 2

Ossie knew the Wilderness was dangerous. He felt it. Smelled it, even. He felt oddly unsettled since having crossed the lake, as if something, somewhere, was watching and waiting.

It was good to be paranoid at moments like these. He was attuned to hate, having endured it as a gay black man in the 20th century. Ossie was prepared for whatever manner of monstrous human possibilities the Wilderness contained, including cannibals, warlords, child soldiers, and death squads.

Except for Mildred Zimer. There was no preparing for a naked old woman walking toward him from out of the trees, with silver hair draped in wiry disarray over her shoulders, and flesh as scarred and spotted as the surface of the moon.

The exiles bunched behind Billy, but he was no better equipped to deal with Mildred Zimer. She stood on the other side of the pit and examined each of them one at a time. A slim smile cut into her wrinkled, sunbaked face.

"Don't panic, please," she called.

More bodies emerged from the woods, elderly men and women, all nude. And without an ounce of shame, like Adam and Eve before the fall. They filed in behind Mildred and spread their ranks around the edge of the pit. Eleven, including Mildred, now stood in a line and watched the exiles watching them.

A woman appeared at the edge of the trees. Light passed through the sheer black robe she wore, illuminating the faint outline of her long, lean figure. She was younger than the others. On Earth, Ossie would have guessed mid to late forties but age was meaningless on the Island. Her curly black hair swept over intense and curious blue eyes. Her gaze fell either on Billy or

Sophia, Ossie couldn't tell which.

Some of the nudists smiled warmly, trying to disarm the tension among the exiles. Others were somber, measuring the new arrivals carefully.

"We are the Engineers," Mildred continued. "We are here to welcome you to the Wilderness."

"I'm not exactly sure what you have in mind," Billy said. "But we aren't interested."

Several of the Engineers chuckled and Mildred cracked a wide grin.

"We certainly understand," Mildred said. "And I assure you, we are quite harmless."

"As long as you behave yourselves," a short old man added. He had a deep, sunken chest and patchy white hair sweeping his arms, his soft pink chest, and sprinkled across his head.

"Okay, you've welcomed us," Billy said. "Thank you, and if you don't mind—"

"New exiles are always such prudes." a short, chubby Engineer beside Mildred said. Basically a bowling ball with skinny legs.

"But we don't want to make a bad impression," Mildred said. "So we will leave you with your housewarming gifts and be on our way."

Mildred motioned to the others. Three broke rank and walked back into the forest.

"We can be great friends," Mildred said. "We don't ask for anything more than loyalty and, as Philip mentioned, that you behave yourselves. We are not interested in land, power, or worshipers. We just like the Wilderness to remain a nice, quiet place to live."

The Engineers returned, carrying large fabric bags and a backpack.

"Tents, lighters, flashlights," Mildred said. "Just some things to get you started. The Wilderness is abundant, so there is no need to fight or steal. If you need it, come to us and we will supply it.

"Do you work with Bali?" Sophia asked.

"Sometimes," Mildred said, her eyes resting on Sophia. "You have grown up so pretty, my dear. We were very worried about you."

Sophia frowned. Her hand found Billy's and their fingers laced tightly.

Mildred looked at Ossie. Several heartbeats passed as the two watched one another.

"Interesting," Mildred said to herself.

A tall woman beside Mildred leaned close and whispered as both of them watched Ossie. Mildred nodded.

"If you need anything else, do not hesitate to ask," Mildred said by way of goodbye. The other Engineers turned and walked back into the forest. The woman in the sheer robe paused and looked at Sophia, revealing a slight and devious smile. Ossie looked at Sophia, who met the woman's eyes. The woman bowed her head and retreated into the forest.

Mildred stood alone.

"Why didn't you come to me when I was exiled?" Edward asked.

"Tommy," Mildred replied.

Edward didn't ask her to explain. He was afraid of what she might say.

"You wouldn't happen to have a piano, would you?" Raul asked.

"Not at the moment, but we may be able to scare something up for you. Give us a few weeks to work on it."

"Really? How do we find you?" Raul asked.

"We find you," Mildred replied, then turned to follow the

others.

After the Engineers were back within the woods, Billy circled the pit to reach the Engineers offerings. He knelt down, opened the backpack, and looked inside. He dropped it, grabbed a bag and opened it.

"What's in there?" Todd asked.

"Camping equipment, mostly," Billy said.

"That was quite a welcoming committee," Ossie offered, but no one laughed.

Petrov the Painter
Part 3

Petrov moved the female head from the work room before beginning, leaving her on a pillow in his room. He later regretted facing her toward his wife's mural. Petrov was always bad about those sorts of things.

She was glad to have his art to look at, though. It was a good way of getting to know the renowned artist, a man who had been widely discussed from the moment he arrived on the Island.

She'd seen his paintings, murals, and of course the painted skulls, which decorated the homes of the most prominent Americans. She'd wished for a chance meeting with the artist, to discuss the sad eyes, the high and elegant cheekbones, the angry suns. She wanted to convince him to paint her something, anything, as small as a stick drawing on scrap paper. She just wanted a record of his genius.

And now she was in his bedroom, staring at the mural dominating the bunker and, she assumed, his heart.

In the workroom, Petrov lifted one of the male heads from the pillow, then leaned its forehead against his. He muttered a prayer to a god he no longer worshiped. On the workbench sat the other male head, faced away by Petrov so it couldn't see its fate.

Petrov stood and approached the metal drum. His gloves crinkled loudly as he worked the crowbar under the lip of the drum lid. The steel squealed as the lid pried off.

Petrov turned, retrieved a cloth face mask from a shelf, and fixed it over his face. He gently picked up the head.

"Are you ready, my friend?" Petrov asked. It blinked "yes".

Petrov lowered the head into the acid. A pungent steam

billowed up around it where the acid boiled. The head's face contorted in pain, mouth gaping in a silent scream. Its eyes fluttered, its jaws locked, muscles spasmed. The acid ate away its cheeks, nearing its mouth, rushing into the skull and cleaning out the brain matter. The eyes sagged open, lifeless. The pain eclipsed the nightmare of the Island.

Petrov leaned over the vat as he submerged the skull completely. A final tuft of hair detached from the skull and floated, briefly. The steam subsided as bubbles belched out the stench of scorched flesh. The cleaned skull dripped acid as Petrov lifted it from the vat. The sun would later bleach the red stain from the skull, preparing the canvas for Petrov's new masterpiece.

Petrov placed the skull in the shadows. Then he walked around to face the remaining head, the eyes open with terror. Petrov would give this one more time, he decided. He would pray with the condemned man, let him find peace before leaving the last of his body behind.

***

She watched Petrov eat a bowl of stew, searching his face, wishing the quiet man would talk more. When he noticed her, she rose her eyebrows, flagging his attention.

"I'm sorry, are you hungry?" Petrov asked, knowing it was a ridiculous question.

"No."

"It must be hard for you to watch this," Petrov said, placing his spoon down and standing. "I will finish in the other room."

"No."

Petrov settled back into his seat.

"I have never been good with company," Petrov began, now too uncomfortable to resume his meal. "I had—"

Petrov hesitated, then picked up the spoon and immediately

placed it back down.

"I had a daughter who would talk when we had guests. My wife and I never talked because we did not need to. Not with Mayla around."

He lifted the spoon again, forced some stew into his mouth, and chewed as quickly as he could. When he'd finished it and used a napkin to clear his beard, he carried the bowl to the kitchen and put it in the sink with the other dirty plates.

Petrov paused in the doorway to the kitchen and watched the head. She stared back into his eyes, so curious about the odd painter. If only he would talk.

"Did you have children?" Petrov asked.

"Yes."

"Ah," Petrov replied with a nod. Moments passed. "How many."

"One. Two. Three. Four."

"Wow, so many!" Petrov smiled. "I could not even handle two daughters. Or a wife, for that matter."

Petrov laughed softly. The head smiled. Silence resumed.

"Would you like to watch me work?" Petrov asked.

"Yes."

Thankful, Petrov retrieved the head, wound through darkened concrete tunnels, the head glancing into every opened room, counting the doors (5), the steps (34), anything to engage in the moment. Petrov reached a blast door in the rear of the bunker. He unlatched the heavy door and pushed it outward, exposing an open area filled with art supplies and tinted solar panels in large, gleaming rectangles tilted towards various breaks in the trees to capture energy throughout the sun's path across the sky. Five inverted parasols sprouted from the earth for rain capture funneling down to tanks below ground. A long, domed, brick kiln stretched ten feet across with a chimney raising out of the back.

Petrov pulled a work bench over to the kiln and carefully placed the head's pillow on top, then eased her down on the satin.

"I must prepare the wood early," Petrov explained. "I can only burn at night so the children across the lake can't see the smoke. If the night is too clear, the angels will tell me to stop."

Petrov retrieved chopped wood from a large pile, opened the hatch and tossed the wood deep into the kiln. He turned and faced the head.

"She is my wife," Petrov said. "The mural in my bedroom. If it bothers you, I can cover it."

"No."

Petrov smiled at her. Their eyes lingered on one another's as they softly tumbled towards love.

I Cannot Die
Part 4

Hell is an eternally breaking heart. The great absence. Like the darkness beyond the reaches of our universe, Hell is where God does not go. Those of us cast into damnation do not suffer fire, demons, or pitchforks. Only regret. The ideological stands that were so critical in our lives diminish and are replaced with time.

So.

Much.

Time.

Edward the Fallen
Part 3

Edward returned to the shore for his things: the tent, sleeping bag, what was left of the food Tommy scavenged for him. The afternoon wore on as he watched the waves and wept. Above, the plane hummed to and fro, like a bee collecting pollen for the hive.

When would Tommy return? The new camp site was not far away, but Tommy would need to look to find it. Would the boy with ocean eyes bother to seek out his lover, or would he just retreat back into the darkness?

And did Edward really want to be found?

Edward stood and wiped the sand from his shorts, preparing to leave. An explosion rumbled in the distance, drawing Edward's eyes back to the Wilderness. To the forbidden center, where Tommy had fled from love.

A fireball rose high above the canopy, where it formed a mushroom cloud. Dread wound through Edward's guts.

"Breaking your heart," the switchblade woman had told him.

Forever breaking. Edward's heart only knew love to be a temple quickly formed, but doomed to crumble, piece by piece, with the inevitability of time and human frailty.

Edward fell to his knees and watched the fire give way to black smoke, a crooked finger pointing up to the infinite. A hollow panic gripped Edward. He could run, but to where? He could scream, but for who? Tommy was beyond his reach. Dead for good this time, perhaps.

Edward eased his breathing, using meditation instead of prayer. He wiped away his tears, packed his supplies, and returned to the campground where the other exiles discussed the explosion. What was left of the mushroom cloud, barely visible through the canopy, was dissipating in swirls as the angels attempted to sweep the sky clean.

Digging to Heaven

Hauan Tsang never used lamps. He tunneled by sound, smell, and touch, especially when he was burrowing toward Heaven. It was the agreement with the Americans. He built their tunnels; they gave him two days a week to dig into the core of the Island.

Volunteer labor for his pet project was hard to come by. Everyone was scared of falling through the bottom of the world and into the unknown. That is what drove Hauan—the desire to gaze down upon Heaven, to drop from the underbelly of God's creation and fall back into paradise.

He didn't know if he would keep falling forever, if he would be welcomed back into the sea of souls, or if he would fade into nothingness. It was the not knowing that drove him back down into his hole every chance he got.

Sometimes he would find a willing partner or two who were just as curious and daring as he was. But most people's nerves were rattled easily in the suffocating darkness. So when he ran out of thrill seekers, there were always prisoners. For them, a day of digging meant a day out of the ovens.

It was not like the tunnels on Earth when Hauan fled the mines in China for Gam Saan (The Mountains of Gold) in San Francisco. Or Oklahoma City, where he'd settled when xenophobia pushed his people from California into the Midwest. He first settled in the work camps of the emerging downtown, then dug out a home beneath the streets, creating a sprawling complex where the Chinese could live, work, and survive beneath the hateful eyes of the West.

Such perseverance was rare on the Island. The exiles wanted only comfort and shelter from their confused God. Hauan gave that shelter to the Americans in return for forced labor to help him dig to Heaven.

The Americans.

The phrase still turned Hauan's stomach, but they paid well and never interfered with his pet project. The Engineers were the only other power in the Wilderness, but their eyes were always pointed up. They had no use for tunnels. The Engineers did not want empires or homes or court houses or libraries. For all Hauan could tell, the Engineers only wanted to bake in the sun, feast, and fuck. They were like pigs, feral humans with no desire to build a community.

He had never been to their sanctuary, so he considered that his assessment might be unfair. But he'd always been suspicious of mystics.

The Americans weren't mystics; they were pioneers who wanted to expand with the same abandon as they had on Earth. Since they could not build up with glimmering skyscrapers and gaudy mansions, they built down in a sprawling web work of tunnels. The dense vegetation at ground level provided thick roots to hold up earthen ceilings. Because the Island was young, there were few stone veins, and these had not been created through compression, time, and heat. This stone was just an artifice, silted into the Island by God like the last brushstrokes of a painting.

Hauan knew this because, the deeper he got, the fewer veins he found. God couldn't be bothered. It made for easy digging, but also easy tunnel collapses. The tunnelers before Hauan had not understood this, how to compensate for the absence of rock. So many had been buried alive.

And sometimes still are.

A glimmer caught Hauan's eye as he jerked his spade from the earth. Unaccustomed to light, his eyes narrowed as the faint light broke through the dirt. Hauan looked back up toward the surface of the hole, wondering if his laborers were awake and watching. Probably not. A bell dangling beside him in the hole did not ring, as it would if they wanted to communicate, to ask about the mysterious glimmer. Sound was dangerous this deep, so Hauan allowed no sound aside from whispers or the gentle tintinnabulation of the bell.

Hauan glanced back down to the light, brushed away the dirt, then cupped the glowing object. It was soft and malleable like flesh. It was warm. Fluid swished inside from subtle rhythmic beats, almost as if being pumped by a heart.

Hauan wrapped it in a handkerchief and packed it in a knapsack that hung beside the bell. He'd seen the lights before. He'd never spoken to anyone about them. He dealt with the strange objects in his own way.

Hauan resumed digging, piling dirt into buckets, ringing the bell, and waiting for the buckets to ascend and for their replacements to drop. Sometimes the ring brought immediate attention; other times it took the sleeping prisoners time to rouse.

Hours passed as Hauan descended toward Heaven with no idea how deep he would ultimately have to burrow.

The bell rung. Three times. Emergency.

Hauan heard a second rope lowering beside him, like a boa constrictor uncoiling from a tree. He grabbed it and ran his hand along the rope until he found the loop. He stepped into it, rang the bell, and was pulled up toward the surface.

***

Hauan led the prisoners through the dark, winding tunnels for ten minutes before the first daylight appeared. Long, tubular solar lights implanted through the crust of the Island bounced sunlight down into the depths. They lined the tunnels so the less practiced tunnelers could find their way.

Hauan didn't need the light. He could find his way to every vein of the American complex based on the chill of the air, the smell of the distant mudpits, and an internal map more reliable than anything drawn up by the Americans.

They arrived at a new tunnel. It was to be a production facility where the mud would be baked, turning the food into bricks and other building supplies. The Americans always searched for the familiar. Not satisfied with tunnels, they wanted to recreate the true America.

The prisoners held an oil lamp up to a bare wall. The dirt fell away easily, meaning someone had already dug here since the formation of the Island. The light moved along the wall, revealing the strikes of the spade into the earth.

Then moisture dripping thick and smelling of copper. The light moved more, searching.

"There," a worker said.

The light fell on three fingers exposed, the rest of the hand entombed within the earthly wall.

"Well," Hauan whispered. "What are you waiting for?"

The prisoners went to work with hand shovels, carefully digging the dirt away, exposing the hand, then an arm. Slow, methodical work yielded more and more of the body until, finally, a face appeared. A young man, eyes and mouth closed tight. He was lying on his side. Hauan guessed he'd tried to dig himself out, but did not know which way was up. The compression stopped his struggle.

The prisoners continued to dig until the Island yielded the limp body. They pulled him from the dirt and away from the wall.

A prisoner retrieved a book from his knapsack and opened it. He held his lamp up as he flipped the pages.

"Wake him up," Hauan said to the other prisoner, who

unscrewed a canteen and dripped water onto the man's face.

The man's eyes fluttered. His nostrils flared, trying to bring in air. More water was splashed on his face.

The man spasmed and flailed, eyes open. Hauan and one of the prisoners grabbed the man by the arms, forced him back to the ground, and held him there. "Sshh!"

They turned the man over as he began vomiting dirt and maggots. Hauan spun him back around and pried open his mouth. The prisoner poured water inside. They turned him back over and let him vomit again. The process repeated over and over until the man finally settled, exhausted, his eyes gazing into the shadows, his breaths raspy but full as his cleared lungs were able to sustain life again. His lungs would need to be flushed every day for several weeks until they'd be completely clear.

"Your name?" Hauan asked.

The man attempted to talk, but could only make dry, cracked sounds. Hauan motioned to the prisoner. He tipped the canteen gently against the man's lips, letting water dribble into his mouth. It stayed down. The man coughed and licked his lips.

"Walter," he managed. "Coleman."

The second prisoner consulted the book.

"Seven years," the second prisoner announced. "Four others were lost with him."

"Seven years?" the man asked. "This is the Island? Still?"

"Yes, my friend," Hauan said. "You have been in the dirt for seven years, but now you are free."

"Kill me," Walter said. "Please."

Hauan exchanged a look with the prisoner holding the book, then looked back down at Walter.

"Let's find your friends."

Tommy, The Boy With The Beautiful Ocean Eyes

When Tommy disappeared into the Wilderness, he did not intend to be gone for two weeks. He did not even intend on being gone the entire afternoon. He walked and continued walking, passing the pits, passing the trees burdened with ripe apples, past the small huts where food could be traded for a few hours of labor, through the open field of Rawlings, past the security outposts and the stovepipes of ovens that resonated with the hideous screams of the condemned. On he walked, compelled back into the heart of America.

Tommy did not remember a time in his life when he had not been addicted to something or someone. A relapse was not a single, conscious decision for Tommy. Nor was it a series of justifications, but rather something like hypnotism. He felt pulled along toward self-destruction, knowing but not knowing what he was about to do. As he stood at the edge of New Wichita, he did not even think of turning away. He was simply retracing a day that had already happened time and time again. A part of him that was beyond reason had already made the choices.

The forest around New Wichita was particularly dense. The infant American empire hid beneath the Island with only small tubes sprouting up from the soil for light and ventilation.

"Beyond His Eye," was the golden rule of the Island. Everything hidden. Not a lie, not an affront, just discreet.

Like the great westward expansion of North America, New Wichita was hungry to claim the land, to build, to establish the greater society its people believed was their divine right. If they could not build football fields, statues, and shopping malls in the open, then they would establish a subterranean utopia. The

Island's only cavern was claimed first, then came the first homes, the civic buildings, the retail shops, a running track, warehouses for their supplies, and even a bank for their wealth. The ovens served as a jail and were already at capacity.

The library was still awaiting its first submission.

"The books aren't the important part of a library, anyway," the mayor stated at the ribbon-cutting ceremony. The light of the headlamp still strapped to her head blinked out and an aid tapped at it until it flashed back on. "It is our commitment to literacy that is the key."

I would have happily stocked their shelves if only they'd asked.

New Wichita was among just a few subterranean American communities, and its downward expansion was by far the most aggressive.

Every citizen of New Wichita possessed a skill: builder, cook, brewer, butcher, sheriff, seamstress, prostitute. Everyone had a place, everyone had a job to do. The wife of a roofer was even working with a former small engine mechanic to build a printing press in the hopes of starting the first newspaper on the Island. Metal was hard to find, so progress was slow. Trades and bargains had to be struck with me or the Engineers.

Old patterns, recovering the familiar. That was New Wichita. Regardless of what God had intended when He created the Island, the Americans were intent on rebuilding the world they left behind. Sure, Downtown New Wichita was located in the mouth of a cavern which saw sunlight for only four hours each day, but it was a downtown all the same. City Hall, the mayor's mansion, a flagpole that rarely received the gift of wind—all parts of the symbol of civilization. A few of the buildings were even made from wood instead of clay. When God exiled the children and the campground was empty, the Americans would harvest as many trees as they could until the next batch of campers arrived. It was the only time the angels didn't bother silencing the American axes.

The mayor believed that if they continued building, continued sprawling, then God—the God of Plenty—would grant them more. The God of Old America was also the God of New America. She was certain of it.

The Americans embraced Tommy the moment he materialized in the Wilderness. A beautiful man always had a role in New Wichita, especially if that beautiful man understood the value of secrecy. Tommy became a luxury item traded among members of the well-to-do.

"Doesn't this reek of hypocrisy?" Tommy asked the second day in New Wichita. He was sitting on the edge of the judge's bed. A halo of light spilled from a solar tube and bounced off the mirrored walls, so the home felt less like a cave than like the proper home of a dignitary. Tommy heard a distant wail drifting through the tunnels. A convicted homosexual was being cooked in one of the ovens on the outskirts of town, a prolonged torture that would have killed a human on Earth. On the Island, it was only a scalding misery that could last for days, weeks, or months depending on the whims of the council.

Out of sight, but not out of mind. That was punishment the New Wichita way.

"Not at all," the judge said from beneath the covers, his skin still glazed with sweat. Off in the kitchen, his wife could be heard scuttling about and humming something vaguely country-western. Grease popped furiously after she slapped down a slice of real ham on the skillet. Pigs were a brand new development on The Island.

Tommy walked to the outside wall and leaned his forehead against the hardened clay, imagining the ovens, the heat, and the hopelessness.

Each oven burned for one hour a day. He'd never seen the actual ovens, but did see the stovepipes on the surface that let out heat when the condemned were burned.

The screams could be heard clearly throughout the caves as well as on the surface. It was more for the benefit of the townspeople, to remind them that law and order was firmly in place. Most were only condemned to the ovens for a week or two, but one woman had been shut into her oven for over three years. She was no longer burned, just forgotten.

"What is the difference between what he did and what we did?" Tommy asked. The screams were dying out as the burning came to an end.

A dark glare crossed the judge's face. "With what we did last night, there was a woman involved," he answered. Then he swung his feet off the bed and stood to his full, imposing height. "And we will not get caught."

The judge crossed the room from the bed to Tommy. Tommy looked away.

"Right?" the judge asked.

Tommy nodded his head. "Of course."

Later that day, the judge traded Tommy off to the town treasurer, a firm woman who enjoyed a man who listened and withstood. Then came the botanist who was testing vegetation for hallucinatory effects. Tommy was a willing guinea pig. But the days were getting too long. He was too far from home.

Edward was home.

That thought never changed for Tommy. Even as time passed in a blur and he rotated from one bed to the next, a favor for a favor for a favor, Edward remained his home. Edward was where Tommy had left his heart. He would return for it when he was strong enough to carry it again. He just needed another drink to set him right, another night to bleed the sickness from his system, another indulgence to purify his unworthy soul.

Barry and Mary and Domestic Bliss

Fear was a potent aphrodisiac, making sex one of the most important ways Barry and Mary communicated during their first months in the Wilderness. Even as an American hunting party searched the woods, no more than fifty yards away, Barry clutched Mary's hips, bringing her against him, his breath on her neck, her lips tight, trying to stay as quiet as she could.

If the Americans found them, they would be sent to the ovens, maybe even executed. But their love was a cyclone, overwhelming and invincible, harboring no doubt or fear, only spinning foolishly onward.

They didn't plan on becoming outlaws, but fate and boredom had put them at odds with the quick expansion of New Wichita and America's puritanism.

As Barry's focus blurred and his nerves sparked, Mary's eyes opened to watch the darkened woods for the hunting party. She heard distant voices and saw shadows moving, but she waited for Barry, one hand clutching his hair and pulling his face to hers, the other hand gripping a bow strung with the guts of a fallen deer.

It was the first animal she'd ever killed.

Barry's body tightened, trembling. Then the spasms came, and then a stifled gasp. She felt him kiss her earlobe. His weight settled over hers.

"Atta boy," Mary whispered, patting him on the cheek. Barry released her and reached for his spear.

Without a word, Mary slid into black denim jeans and a dark jacket. Barry pulled on jeans and a loose, button-up shirt. Not ideal for hunting, but the clothes were durable and blended with the forest. Work clothes. They could be ruined by the forest.

Barry and Mary knew where they could always get more.

Winded but exhilarated, they fled to the north.

The Americans had been incensed when Barry and Mary broke into their food stores for the third time in a month. The couple didn't steal from the Americans to satiate hunger; they did it to kill the boredom.

"We are alive again!" Mary exclaimed to Barry when he suggested they stop harassing New Wichita. "I will not waste another life waiting for death!"

Barry always relented.

They spent their more leisurely days tucked inside a cave camouflaged by the forest on the far west side of the Island. The cave burrowed into a hill where the warm, healing waters of an underground stream washed away hard hours of foraging.

They choose not to grow crops in fear of divulging their location. Instead, Barry and Mary raided the American food stores when the days grew long. They visited the Engineers each time Barry finished another batch of moonshine for a crazed night of revelry. The strange muck in the pits bubbling up throughout the Island fermented easily. Rather than brewing it into a weak, thick beer as everyone else did, Barry distilled it. Early concoctions tasted like an oily and sweet whiskey, but it did the trick. After he began throwing in fistfuls of raspberries and mint leaves to add character, his moonshine developed a fiery character and became a prized commodity across the Island for its potency and taste. Barry never traded to New Wichita out of principle, so the Americans would go to great lengths to trade with anyone who could get them some of his moonshine.

Barry was using a trade embargo to give the rest of the Wilderness a bit of leverage over the Americans. Like Cuba with its cigars.

If the feral lovers ever were captured, Barry hoped the

promise of moonshine might keep their heads attached to their bodies.

From time to time, Barry worried that he was letting Mary spin too freely, embracing a chaotic life without consequence. She seemed to feel more invincible after every skirmish with the Americans.

And on their latest brush, they'd heard an alarm while they were digging through the dry storage in search of fresh venison, a specialty of New Wichita.

That chase had lasted longer than any of the others, with Barry and Mary skirting around patrols for three straight nights. When twelve townspeople still refused to give up the hunt, Barry insisted that they lead them as far from their cave as possible before slipping them for the last time.

With the night wearing on and sleep deprivation slowing the couple down, they decided a few hours of rest would be sensible. Barry slept first. Mary sat beside him, primping the feathered fletching of an arrow.

The first shadow appeared an hour later as the moonlight mist poured through the tree canopy. The breeze rustled the leaves, hiding the sounds of footfalls. Mary nudged her husband. Barry surfaced from sleep, taking only a moment to adjust to lucidity before reaching for his spear.

More shadows appeared, circling Barry and Mary, preparing to advance. The only break was north. The couple jumped to their feet and bolted through the trees, the hunting party scrambling behind. Spotting the cliffs at the edge of the Island, Barry and Mary broke through the trees. Arrows soared through the vegetation, whistling over their heads, skittering across the rocks in front of them before falling off the edge and down toward Heaven.

The hunting party flanked them and began closing in with

blades drawn and bows pulled taut. Barry turned to face the cliff, considering the leap, assuming the fall would be better than facing decapitation, the stoves, a pike, or something even worse.

Mary grabbed Barry's shirt and pulled him against her, her lips reaching up to his. The desperate kiss muted the Island for a few precious seconds. The hunting party paused, uncertain and uncomfortable as they watched the lovers embrace.

"Don't let them take me," Mary whispered, pushing her bow into his hand along with her last three arrows.

Mary charged the group with a banshee wail and a flint-bladed knife. Barry quickly took up the bow, notched an arrow, and released it over Mary's shoulder. It struck a man in the chest and sent him backward. Barry quickly notched and fired the last two arrows into a woman who'd been aiming her own bow at Mary. Barry dropped the bow, took up his spear, and sprinted toward Mary, who was swinging her knife in manic arcs as the hunting party closed in on her.

Arrows skimmed over Barry's head as he plunged into the melee. Blood from knife strikes spurted like ocean spray into the air. The hunters retreated in pain, terror, and confusion. Barry drove his spear into a man clutching onto Mary's hair. The man screamed in pain as Barry pushed him forward, forcing the others out of the way. Then Barry released the spear, took Mary's hand, and they dashed past the group. As they fled toward the woods, an arrow plunged into Mary's shoulder. She gasped, but kept running.

Of their twelve pursuers, only three were left standing and unscathed. All would live because death was not so easily granted on the Island.

After they had put some distance between themselves and the hunting party, Barry pulled the arrow from Mary's skin and dressed the wound. She'd also gotten cut on the hip and was having trouble walking. Barry carried her for the last leg of the trip. They approached their cave cautiously, but found the tarp and stones hiding the entrance unmolested. Barry cradled Mary all the way to the underground stream. She grimaced as he lowered her into the foaming water. Within moments, the water sealed the wounds and washed away the blood stains. They made love time after time until they were both spent. Mary woke intermittently throughout the night, weeping in a fevered panic. The waters could do nothing for the wounds of the mind.

When morning arrived, Mary rose with an innocent smile. She laughed about their bumbling in the dry storage, their near capture, and the Americans' astonishment that someone was brazen enough to stand up to them.

"Perhaps next time, we should just burn their stupid town down, maybe make off with a few farmer's daughters," she said. "You could have yourself a little harem, would you like that?"

"That sounds terrible," Barry said.

"Correct answer," Mary replied, kissing him on the temple.

Barry knew he should be worried about how feral she was becoming. But it excited him. He didn't push her, but he didn't have any interest in muzzling her.

Mildred arrived later in the day, uninvited but not unexpected. She always knew when Barry and Mary were up to no good and came around to check on their battle scars.

"The rest of your friends have been exiled," Mildred announced, cradling a cup of moonshine.

Barry and Mary glanced at each other nervously. They had avoided visiting Edward because of Tommy. The Americans were expanding further every day and The Engineers would soon be forced to react. A war would likely come, so Barry and Mary took great pains to not get involved and to avoid any dangerous connections. They trusted only each other.

"How are they?" Mary asked.

"Fine," Mildred said. "Edward isn't alone anymore, which is good. The others seem nice. That won't last."

A cringe crept across Mildred's face as she took a sip of the moonshine. It was a rough batch, which is why Barry hadn't traded it.

"Where do you think they will end up?" Mildred asked. "With the Americans, cowering on the shorelines with the fishermen, or as outcasts, like you?"

Mary smirked.

"Or with Simon?" Mildred added.

Barry shook his head, a frigid cloud over his face at the sound of Simon's name. He poured himself more moonshine and rested against the cave wall.

"Maybe they will start something new," Mary said. "With Billy leading, maybe they will change things."

"Doubtful," Mildred replied. "But we can hope."

"Any sign of the Ku Klux Clams?" Barry asked, referencing Martha and her fanatical followers.

"They are finding their own way," Mildred said. "Toward the Americans, I would imagine."

"To the poor Americans," Mary called, raising her cup in a toast. "May they receive those shrews as the blight they so deserve."

They clinked cups and drank. Silence rested on the trio for several minutes until Mary thought of food. She stood without a word and retrieved some of the venison, passing portions to Mildred and Barry.

The moonshine flowed as they drank and thought in silence.

"That boy is an infestation," Mildred grumbled suddenly, eyes dimmed from the alcohol. Barry and Mary knew she was talking about Simon. "He's an infestation more insidious than the Americans."

Barry and Mary didn't reply. They still had fond feelings toward the young magician and admired how boldly he stood against God's authority. But they had heard stories. Something in Simon must have changed when he abandoned the campground.

"We will have to burn the Island from coast to coast to finally be rid of him," Mildred announced. "Or until he is rid of us."

Tommy The Boy With The Beautiful Ocean Eyes
Part 2

Darkness is a flash flood. Tommy smelled the storm approaching long before the clouds rose from the horizon in their slow, tumbling crawl. The rains were warm and cleansing when they started. But soon the rushing waters swelled, threatened, overwhelmed, and swept Tommy away. There was no swimming against the current, no banks to struggle towards. There was only submission. Tommy's terror and his weakness, his confusion and his pain, all of it pushed Tommy forward. The days passed as a dreary fog, each night a mania of sensation. Flesh, alcohol, fury, theft, submission. Tommy only retained flashes until the darkness passed.

And it finally did. Tommy was numb, his breath easy for the first time in two weeks as he awoke in the soft bed of The Mayor of New Wichita.

Tommy felt restored. His chest had hollowed out, the confusion cleared, leaving ample room for his heart to beat life back into his body. That body, though weary, battered, and spent, would carry him home.

Home to Edward.

The bed creaked as a naked body turned beside him, pulling the sheet with it. Light poured in from a large window where the sunrise cracked through the mouth of the downtown cavern. It was like waking in the mouth of a whale.

The body moved again and Tommy made out the spine and narrow hips of a man hidden by the sheet. A second body slid against Tommy and a woman's hand emerged to caress his chest. Neither body belonged to The Mayor.

Tommy eased the hand off his chest and inched to the foot of the bed. He glanced over the side and peered into the dark bedroom. As always, he found his clothes folded beside the bed. It was a trick he'd picked up during his time as a male escort in Los Angeles to ensure a quick getaway.

Like the skilled tradesman he was, Tommy dressed quickly and quietly and carried his shoes as he tiptoed to the bedroom door. He heard high heels clicking against wood flooring with short, firm, and purposed footsteps. Tommy knew it was The Mayor before she appeared in the doorway.

"You," The Mayor snapped in a hushed whisper. She wore a wrinkled business suit. Tommy had known she would not make it home last night, having watched her steal away to the home of the Island's only banker after a council meeting. That meant the mansion would be empty for the night, a perfect place to crash for one last night in America.

He hadn't thought about when she would return. When mania hit, he never thought of mornings.

The Mayor's face was sharp, like that of so many wealthy wives Tommy used to entertain on Earth. Easy marks, most of them, desperate for attention, revenge, or validation. Sex was a business agreement for them, an act of war, a way of assuming power in an unbalanced marriage.

Tommy knew to smile and absorb no matter what they said or did. They always paid. They always tipped.

The Mayor was an excellent lay but a terrible lover. The difference was as lost on her as it had been lost on her late husband. To say she was jealous to see Tommy with other lovers wouldn't be entirely correct, but she was territorial.

Tommy offered a sheepish smile.

The Mayor leaned her head into the room, examining the bodies still sleeping in the bed. Tommy could tell she was trying to match the body parts to names. Then she spun and marched away, snapping her fingers at Tommy, commanding him to follow like an obedient dog.

He did. It was all part of her game.

***

Mirrors were the great luxury of New Wichita. The Mayor's mansion gleamed with hundreds of them set into clay walls, tilted to bounce light throughout the halls and rooms. Tall, body-length mirrors, clusters of small circular mirrors positioned like solar systems, long mirrors running along opposite walls of a hallway to make the space look immense. The image of The Mayor striding ahead of Tommy in the hallway bounced back and forth between the opposing mirrors for an eternity. Tommy laughed as he watched a million other Tommys hop on one foot to slip on a shoe.

They turned into the front sitting room where twin twelve-foot windows welcomed the sunrise shining in through the maw of the cavern. A Petrov mural depicting the persecution and crucifixion of Jesus wrapped the room's walls. Grim and bloody, it faced the open mouth of the cavern, as if The Mayor hoped that God would peer in one day and be pleased. Little clay sculptures were the only decoration in the otherwise sparse room.

The Mayor had ordered the architect to emulate the Southern Gothic estates that survived the emancipation, like a grand plantation house that had been swallowed whole by the earth. The wooden and stone facade had been cut into the cavern wall with gaping windows to capture the brief hours of sunlight afforded to the cavern entrance. The most ambitious building project so far on the Island, The Mayor's mansion dwarfed the emerging City Hall, which barely managed two stories and a modest, half-finished dome built with bricks made with mud from the pits.

"How did you get in?" The Mayor asked as she sat down on a velvet fainting chair and kicked off her heels. She'd procured the chair from the Engineers years before in a trade for a small work force to help build a small temple on the eastern edge of the Island.

"You don't lock your windows," Tommy replied. His hangover intensified by the minute, like a waking giant yawning and stretching inside his skull. He eased himself down to the foot of The Mayor's chair, facing her with an intimate smile he hoped would annoy but charm her.

"You are trying to get a rise out of me," she said. "But I am civil, despite what you people say about me."

He stifled the bitter hatred before it rose to his face. He was used to flirting with those he despised.

Tommy's hand slid to her knee. "I don't know what you are talking about."

The Mayor brushed his hand away and stood. She walked across the room to a mirror, then fingered stray hairs back into place. "Oh, you people, the fishers, the outliers, the free spirits who aren't interested in colonizing this land. I've heard what you say about me, about New Wichita and our ways."

"How is your wardrobe coming?" Tommy asked.

The Mayor turned and raised her eyebrow at him. It was a dangerous question, particularly from a prostitute.

"Now, that's not playing fair," she said. "You straighten up or I might have to start playing dirty."

A stranger might have taken the comment as flirtatious, but Tommy knew what it meant. She walked to him, traced her fingers along his cheeks and touched the edge of his lower lip.

"Perhaps it's time for you to find your way back to the lake, you beautiful little boy." She slapped his face a little too hard.

He winced, took a moment to collect himself, then forced a smile.

"I think you may be right." Tommy stood and faced the window, looking up toward the blue sky and the reddish-yellow orb peeking into the cavern. "Quite a view. You can almost see salvation from here."

The Mayor walked up behind Tommy, looking over his shoulder.

"You're not going to find salvation in the sky," she said. "Not anymore."

Tommy chuckled, turned to The Mayor, and stepped in close. Her eyes narrowed; she playfully tilted her face away.

"One more for the road?" Tommy asked.

"Well, aren't you a handful?"

Their eyes were steady, daring one another. Hers flinched first, moving away. She didn't wilt for anybody. Not anymore. She pushed him away and looked to the mouth of the cave. Tommy followed her gaze. A great shadow was emerging. A fog tumbled into the cave, choking out the light. A chill swept over him. Then the smoke dissipated and the shadow was gone.

"What the hell was that?" the Mayor asked.

Tommy was through the front door before the Mayor turned around. There was no time to waste. He had to leave America. He knew that when blackness swept in, Simon came with it.

Barry and Mary and Domestic Bliss
Part 2

"Mary, Mary quite contrary. How does your garden grow?"

Mary dashed behind a tree, then used her hands and a wicker basket to awkwardly hide her nakedness. She couldn't sense the direction of the boy's voice. It seemed to envelope the forest like a breeze, sweeping in from everywhere and nowhere.

"With silver bells and cockle shells," the voice whispered into her ear.

Mary dove from the tree, rolled across the ground behind another wicker basket filled with apples, snatched up her bow and arrow, and aimed into the empty trees.

"And so your garden grows," the voice called, then unleashed a giddy laugh.

"Where are you?"

Footsteps drew her aim to the left, finding Barry, also nude. Mary swept her sight across the trees, looking for a target.

Another shrill boy's laugh. Taunting.

"What's happening?" Barry called, just over a whisper.

"You can't hear him?" Mary asked.

"I don't go whispering in men's ears," the boy's voice replied. A soft breath swept against her earlobe and she jerked away, swinging the bow around to find more empty forest.

"Baby, we're alone," Barry said, slowly approaching Mary.

"It's Simon."

Barry's face hardened. He ran for a spear leaning against a tree. But before he reached it, it swept into the air and spun around, as if it was alive. It hurtled straight at Barry and then stopped, hovering in midair, its point settling only inches away from Barry's eyes like a curious predator.

"What do you want, Simon?" Mary asked.

"To congratulate the happiest couple on the Island. You've reminded us all of the power of true love."

Barry grabbed for the spear, but it danced away, out of reach, then weaved back and forth, shaking its tip as if to say "no." The wind picked up, carrying Simon's laughter with it. This time, Barry heard it.

"The wolves will be out today, you darling lovers!" Simon's now distant voice called. "So run away, you two! Run away!"

The wind died. Mary relaxed her bow and unnotched the arrow. "We have to get back to the cave."

***

They sat quietly on the sturdy branch of an oak, one of the tallest in the Wilderness. They looked eastward over a vast forest stretching for miles beyond New Wichita until yielding to the lake. They waited as the afternoon sun dipped below them in a controlled retreat to the horizon. Mary leaned her head back against Barry, his arms laced around her.

The cave was a short sprint away. Safety.

"Oh my god," Mary gasped.

A fireball bloomed and rose from the largest hill in the Wilderness that marked the cavern of new Wichita.

The blast wave swept over the trees like a wind, but weakened by distance. As it reached Barry and Mary, it was just a subtle thump against their chests. Mary could make out debris flying through the air: stone, tree branches, and dark, limp forms that were probably human body parts.

"Simon," Barry whispered. "What did you do?"

The couple dropped down from the tree and ran to their hidden cave to wait out whatever storm was coming.

The Girl Who Doomed God

It began with the pretty girl who thought she was so fucking clever.

"A Gnat?" the girl said.

"Anat."

"A Gnat?" the girl repeated, wanting to ensure the other new arrivals caught the joke.

Anat dropped her eyes and walked to the runway as the Cessna returned from Heaven with the final batch of kids.

Children exhausted Anat. Groups exhausted her. Idle conversation exhausted her. She'd grown up an isolated child, picking her friends and lovers carefully, drawing them into her life in rations. As she grew into adulthood, she worked to become more comfortable in crowds, but noise overwhelmed her. Concerts were unbearable. Art exhibits, sporting events, any gathering where more than four conversations happened at once—it made her brain overfull. The panic would hit and she would flee. More than once, her friends had found her walking along the side of a road miles from home.

So, no, she wasn't a people person.

But she was loyal.

To her friends.

To her loveless marriage.

To those she admired.

To those she despised.

As much as she detested crowds, Anat thrived on community. She was a poor fit for the campground, but there was hope that she could do well in the Wilderness where isolation was easily found and love could be had at a distance. That was the kind of love at which she excelled.

"Look!" a boy's voice shouted.

Anat turned to see the boy pointing across the Island and up to the sky to a rising mushroom cloud.

Behind the children, the airplane's tires squealed on the asphalt. It bounced as it settled to the ground, steadily slowing. I walked out onto the runway as a door opened and tipped down to reveal stairs up to the cabin. Inside, I cataloged the drowsy new arrivals until I heard panicked squawks from the angels in the cockpit. I scooted past the startled children toward the angles. Through the cockpit window, I saw the mushroom cloud through the front windshield.

Simon had waited until I was off the Island. That clever brat.

The shock wave swept across the Island, only a low rumble this far out. I noticed a shimmer of light out of the corner of my periphery. I looked across the runway and the children gawking up at the cloud. My eyes settled on Anat. She'd folded her arms tightly around her chest and closed her eyes. Whatever light I saw was gone, but I felt something emanating from her. Something more than just panic.

I descended the stairs from the plane and, in my mind, called for all the angels of the Island. I instructed them to dissipate the mushroom cloud and survey the damage. I opened my eyes to see Anat on the edge of the runway. She was glaring at me as the rest of the children watched the skies. She turned away.

I walked to Anat and reached out a hand to her shoulder.

The moment my fingertip touched her, a force erupted. It launched me backwards into the air. I tumbled for fifteen feet, then slammed to the ground. I pushed myself onto my elbows and looked up at Anat. Her skin glowed red. She met my eyes, terrified, then sprinted for the woods. I tried to stand, but the same invisible force that had thrown me into the air now slammed me to the ground, pinning me there until Anat disappeared.

"Great," Jay grumbled from behind me. "We have another one."

I Cannot Die
Part 5

I loved many men and women during my time on Earth. I saw little difference between the sexes beyond a general temperament and physical mechanics. Love is an agonized binding, defiant of sense and formula. My heart seized upon what it seized upon, with little input from my mind or human qualifications.

There was no immortal love, no queen of damnation beside my throne in Hell. There was only a string of devastating and beautiful wounds, the scars of which I still carry today. Though mad love is not singular to mankind, humans elevated it to art beyond reason, beyond instinct, and beyond survival. Humans embraced the totality of the heart's destructive power. God and His angels could only witness it in awe.

Yes, there were many lovers. Thousands—tens of thousands, really—but I do have my favorite. Her name was Hiu-Ying. She lived and died in a prosperous village in an area later known as Kowloon Tong, Hong Kong.

She married early to a wealthy mercantile entrepreneur and shameless social climber. Quiet, beautiful, and clever, Hiu-Ying maintained many lovers. At one point, her lack of discretion tortured her husband to the point that he beat her. Or he attempted to, I should say. When the doctor was summoned, he found the man bleeding profusely from his groin. He would never be able to father children.

Hiu-Ying's husband trembled when she raised her voice to him, but she did this only in private. She knew she'd thoroughly domesticated him and thus had no interest in further humiliating him. She did love him, in her own way, much the same as she loved her dog. They both came and went on her terms.

Hiu-Ying was strong, but she hungered for adoration. She bedded artists, poets, philosophers, anyone with the words and images to adequately mirror her grand reflection. I, having had thousands of years of practice, kept her affections longer than any other man, and she rewarded my praise with absolute submission in the bedroom. Her walls tumbled, her pride faded, and she became mine. An unquestioning surrender, if only for a few hours.

It was two glorious years of sneaking through servant entrances and climbing through windows like a lowly thief just to reach here bed. I'd never been happier.

But then she banished me from her life.

I begged her. That was my mistake. I wanted to own her completely, until the end of her life, but no man owned Hiu-Ying.

By the time she died forty years later, I'd written her 1,481 love letters. Pleadings, exaltations, promises, negotiations, tormented wailing. Each one went unanswered, unless you count her brief smiles when we passed in public.

She was still absorbing my love, so I vowed to shower her until I lost her to the afterlife.

She kept my letters in a trunk which she ordered to be burned upon her death. I was the one who lit the kindling, then watched the evidence of a glorious and excruciating love swept up, ashen, into the ether.

Ours was my most perfect love. I never sought her out in Hell.

How To Properly Manage A Young Empire

What came before New Wichita was of no relevance to The Mayor. Like so many jobs she'd held, it was just more items on a resume, skills earned, lessons learned. But today, on the Island, that was what was real.

Only her most inner circle called her "Katherine" and only in private. To most everyone else, she was "The Mayor." She would also accept "Ma'am." But to her lovers she preferred to be nameless. If they needed to call her something, she requested that it be something coarse and unseemly. Anger helped her orgasm.

Tommy, the beautiful whore, was usually welcome in her bed, but he'd helped himself to her home while she was gone. He'd even left a pair of dazed lovers in his wake. It was enough to justify the ovens for all three of them, but The Mayor couldn't bear the thought of that beautiful face burning. It was hard enough for her to think of him in another person's bed.

Coveting a whore. She was disgusted with herself.

After Tommy left, The Mayor shooed the bodies out of the bed and into the streets. She knew them both and directed them to find their respective ways home as discreetly as possible. A chef and a machinist were not easy to replace, so they would be forgiven as long as they held their tongues.

The public face of New Wichita was moral and driven by entrepreneurship. She did not like the ovens, but they were a bargain with the more rigid members of the community who screamed for executions. Freaks and homosexuals could not, of course, be openly permitted. She understood that, she fully believed in the dangers that an "open" society could pose for the burgeoning community. Liberality was a luxury New Wichita could not yet afford. But with strong, consistent leadership, maybe one day that would change.

The Mayor stripped the bed and left the sheets in a pile for the maid. She knew she should get to work, but opted for an early tumbler of moonshine—young, sweet, and bracing, but effective. She was satisfied with the generosity she had shown Tommy, allowing him to leave when so many Americans were clamoring for his head.

It had been a memorable two weeks for the pretty young man.

"He is a stray that must be put down," the city's arms engineer had said at the previous night's council meeting. They met in the Bullpen, the largest room in New Wichita, located in City Hall. It was formed like a crater, but with an earthen ceiling covering all but a small hole through which light poured down onto a raised stage. All around were four levels of raised platforms with seats that had been chiseled out of stone. Torches cast dancing shadows on the stone walls behind the last row, where an unfinished mural stretched halfway around the circular room. Petrov had been working on it since his arrival, illustrating the history of New Wichita starting with The Mayor's claim of the land and continuing through the construction of the downtown business district inside the mouth of the Great Cave.

The mural was the reason the Americans spoiled Petrov like a kept lover.

On the stage, the council members sat around a long table with The Mayor at the head, watching them bicker. The arms engineer, Walter, was using Tommy's tour through the bedrooms of the community to distract from the growing criticism of his own inability to find a substitute for gunpowder. If they could not replicate even 19th-century weaponry, the Americans would continue to be out-gunned by the mystical Engineers who dominated the Wilderness. The Mayor agreed that Tommy's behavior was disruptive, but not so much that he should be executed. She promised to handle the matter personally.

She wished that all of the freaks were like Petrov, quiet, productive, and submissive. Artists, prostitutes, musicians, and community advocates had their place.

Just not within the borders of New Wichita.

Rabia was the only artist New Wichita could stand. The frail woman was an Egyptian Coptic Christian on Earth and a gifted architect who was responsible for the development of downtown. Rabia retained many nervous habits from her previous life, like reaching to her face for the eyeglasses she expected to be there. But there were no eyeglasses on the Island nor a need for them since everyone possessed 20/20 vision. Or better.

Rabia didn't speak often yet The Mayor sensed her dissatisfaction with New Wichita justice. Rabia held her tongue and delivered projects on or ahead of deadline. When executions were discussed, Rabia would begin rocking back and forth. Subtly. She would never speak, but her nervousness was telling.

The Mayor considered Rabia one of a few potential enemies on the council that may need to be dealt through intimidation or leverage before they gathered the courage to speak against her.

"Politics is anticipation," her uncle once told her. He had been a sheriff. A corrupt sheriff if the papers were to be believed.

A firm knock rattled the door, nearly causing her to tip her drink. She surveyed herself in a full-length mirror near the kitchen, left her drink on the stone counter, and walked to the front door.

"Simon!" was all Hillary could manage, breathless. New Wichita's would-be newspaper baroness was flushed from sprinting to The Mayor's mansion from downtown. Any shred of news sent Hillary into a frenzy, as it would any person whose industry was disaster and gossip.

And Simon's arrival to New Wichita was front page-worthy news, provided the printing press was up and running.

"Where?" The Mayor asked brusquely, closing her front door behind her. The sun had long since passed above the cavern's entrance, leaving only blue skies with a few wisps of clouds. Downtown stretched out along both sides of The Mayor's mansion, running the length of the cavern for a half mile.

Thick black smoke swirled and churned like rushing water along the cavern floor. Construction workers, pedestrians, and a handful of deputies crowded on the stone steps of City Hall, afraid to let the smoke touch them. Inside the cloud, a chorus of voices sang with a ghostly hollowness.

The song wasn't a hymn, but a relic The Mayor recognized from her life on Earth sitting in the backseat of her first boyfriend's Camaro sharing a fifth of Southern Comfort. The song was Black Sabbath's "War Pigs."

As more townspeople arrived from the tunnels, some ran back into the guts of the Island, but most stayed to watch, transfixed by Simon's power.

The Mayor approached City Hall with timid steps, watching the smoke as if it were a feral animal.

"Go home!" The Mayor said. "Go home, you miserable brat!"

She turned to address her people at the edges of the swirling smoke.

"Go back to work! He is all tricks. This is what he wants, to disrupt our lives! Get back to work and he will leave us alone!"

The black smoke drifted to the ground and dissipated, amplifying the voices and revealing the figures within. They stood in a tight group. Simon, still a boy, howled in a beautiful falsetto at the center. Two grown women and one man stood with him, all dressed in long priest's cassocks with upside-down crucifixes made of sticks hanging from necklaces strung with small bones. Inverted black crosses were painted on their faces with ash. Their praying hands were bound together by rosaries strung together with cheap lettered beads. Simon's read "Porn Star".

He was the only child ever to enter the Wilderness, refusing to accept maturity. He hadn't aged a day since his arrival.

"This is not funny!" The Mayor said as she strode to the group, stopping just before Simon. His devilish eyes looked up to hers.

The singing continued:

"Now in darkness world stops turning
Ashes where the bodies burning
No more war pigs have the power
Hand of God has struck the hour
Day of judgment, God is calling."

The Mayor slapped Simon. The boy's head jerked away. Behind him, his followers voices hushed as they watched in horror. Simon looked back to her, a red mark on his face, his crocked smile confident.

"Now, you made me do that," The Mayor said, forcing composure. "Please leave us."

Simon's mouth jerked open and black smoke tumbled out. It swirled around the performers. Hillary screamed and the crowd backed away. The smoke billowed outward, covering the town square and drifting up the cavern's mouth until it blocked the sky. Simon's laugh chirped out from the darkness. Lightning flashed inside the smoke, the crackle of energy echoing through the stone walls.

The smoke advanced toward City Hall like a living thing. The townspeople dashed away, some ducking into buildings, others retreating to the tunnels. A handful remained at The Mayor's side too stunned to move.

The smoke wrapped around City Hall's facade, then broke apart in the middle like theater curtains to expose Simon and his followers rushing up the steps and into the guts of the building. The remaining crowd inched forward, but nobody spoke.

"We demand the release of all prisoners of New Wichita!" Simon called. "God granted us this land to be free, not to be shackled in the tyranny of the past!"

Workers flooded out the front door of City Hall, screaming as they rushed down the steps, keeping their distance from Simon, then ducking away from the smoke as they joined the crowd. The Mayor made a show of waving them behind her. The leader, the mother wolf. Simon's eyes never left her.

"We don't negotiate with terrorists!" The Mayor shouted as the last of the workers trickled out of the building. She got a little thrill from the way the line shot from her mouth. She looked over her townspeople, satisfied with herself.

"Correct," Simon responded. "There will be no negotiation. You will simply do as I ask."

The smoke enveloped Simon and his followers, then swept through the town square. It settled near the general store. Simon stepped from the cloud and addressed the crowd.

"Now is when you run!" he called.

The smoke fell back over him and his followers, then carried them out of the mouth of the cavern.

"Move back!" The Mayor said, then began waving the townspeople away.

Sparks erupted from the open doors of City Hall and showered out across the front steps.

"Run!" Hillary screamed. The crowd sprinted off in all directions.

The Mayor stood her ground, watching their symbol of justice exhale a bloom of color like a fireworks display.

Then it exploded.

Its shock wave hit her chest and lifted her off the ground.

Windows all across the town square shattered. The ceiling above City Hall cracked, sending earth tumbling down from a hole that expanded as more rock and dirt poured into the town square.

The Mayor's eyes were glazed as she looked at the smoke pouring up into the sky. The Island began raining down, the cavern ceiling yielding, crumbling. She gasped just as her face was buried, dirt and stone filling her mouth. She was not scared, only confused.

***

A slow, hard thump in her chest woke The Mayor. She couldn't move, couldn't even open her eyes. It took her several minutes to remember that she was buried alive. Her thoughts were too scrambled to allow for terror. More time passed. She realized that she could wiggle the fingers on her right hand. Even this small bit of freedom comforted her. When she tried moving her lips, she felt the dirt packed into her mouth.

She could not breathe.

Her body spasmed. Fear shouldered its way through her foggy mind. Her limbs strained against the weight. Pain shrieked from the torn skin and shattered bones, but still only her fingers moved. She tried to scream, but her lungs could not gather the air.

She finally gave up, her thumping heart slowing back down. Her fear settled into a manageable dread. She yearned for unconsciousness to escape the reality of her grave, but her mind wouldn't let her.

She focused on the explosion and the cave-in. She tried to guess how much of the ceiling had fallen on her to determine how deeply she was buried.

They were digging now, she told herself. They would unearth her soon. She could not die this way, the Island wouldn't allow it; she merely had to be patient.

There were workers she'd sent into the tunnels years before who still had not been found, but they were laborers. She was the mayor. They would find her.

They will find me.

They will find me.

They will find me.

***

Moisture dripped against her lips. She ignored it, not wanting to wake, not wanting to feel the dirt in her mouth, to remember she could not breathe, could not swallow, could not move her chest.

Her equilibrium shifted, her balance had been disrupted. She slept again.

Something touched her skin. Something that wasn't dirt and stone. Fingers.

Her body flailed, she woke to a sensory storm.

Light.

Sound.

Hands gripping her.

Water pouring against her face.

Her stomach lurched.

Sick mud seeped from her mouth.

Violent coughing.

Oxygen.

She felt unconsciousness returning, the world evaporating.

"Drink more," a voice said.

She knew the voice. A man. His face almost taking shape in the turmoil of her mind.

"Drink more."

She opened her eyes, but was blind. She felt more water splashing against her face. Light glimmered as the dirt washed away but her sight was still too murky to distinguish. She feared she would never see again.

"Drink."

She opened her mouth. The water swirled in, mixing with the dirt and making mud. She gagged, then turned over to vomit again. Finally, the water could reach her stomach. Energy and feeling sparkled through her limbs.

She tried to speak, but her dry lips and bruised lungs failed her.

"Easy, drink more."

It was Hauan. She knew his voice. Of course he'd been the one to find her.

Her lips moved again, managing a thin and dry sound.

She coughed. More water flowing down her lungs. She swallowed hard, feeling strained muscles along her throat.

She tried again.

"How long?"

"Three hours."

The Mayor relaxed into Hauan's arms.

"I will reward you," she said, feeling sleep returning. She resisted with the last of her strength. "We need guns. Tell Walter that we need guns."

"I will."

Darkness retook her.

The Girl Who Doomed God
Part 2

Anat found God on a dirt path overgrown with weeds and encroaching tree branches. She did not know where she was going; she just knew she needed space. She flinched when she saw The Old Man, who wore a yellow and black-striped Stryper T-shirt, heavily starched Wrangler jeans, and running shoes.

Anat slowed and ducked her head as she passed God, not recognizing her Creator and desperate to create distance from everything and everyone until her panic ebbed. God watched her pass, considering, but said nothing.

He continued down the path, sighed, and turned back to the girl.

"I am God!" He called, but she didn't turn around. She didn't even slow.

"I am God!" He repeated, louder and with more authority.

Anat stopped, stiffened, but refused to turn around. "Okay. Can I go now?"

She heard Him breathing. There was a slight wheeze. She wondered if God could be asthmatic. She then heard Him take a step toward her.

"Please don't," Anat said, her back still facing the Creator.

"Don't what?" God asked.

"Whatever it is that you want, just don't."

"I'm not here to hurt you, child," God said, taking another step.

"Stop," Anat insisted, her voice cold.

Heat rose from within her. Leaves from nearby trees began to smolder.

This stopped God. He was not afraid. He was fascinated.

Leaves on the trees around Him ignited and dripped like hellfire from the branches. God took another cautious step toward Anat. She turned her head and addressed God with her dark eyes.

"Don't."

God studied her, took another step forward.

Flames erupted across the trees and bushes as a blast of heat pulsed outward, hitting God. He held out his hand, trying to block the force, but the heat enveloped Him. It singed the gray hairs on His arm and blackened the skin on His palm. His clothes began steaming as He grimaced. She turned toward Him, then sent a pulse of heat outward in all directions. God staggered and struggled to keep on His feet. An inferno spread out into the forest.

The heat subsided. Anat turned back away from God. God waved his hand, squelching the fires.

"Go," God told Anat.

Without a reply, she walked on, disappearing down the trail.

God heard footsteps approaching, so turned to find me on the path. I looked over his charred T-shirt and blackened forearms. I was too stunned to talk.

God pushed past me and stormed toward the airfield. Torn between the child and God, I decided to follow God, catching up just as He approached the Cessna. The children were gathered in a group, Jay waiting for God to address them. God didn't even look their direction as He reached the plane, scaled the steps, and disappeared inside.

The steps folded up, the door closed, and the propellers spun to life. The plane rolled forward, then turned to the opposite direction. I motioned for Jay to come to me and quietly explained what happened as our Creator's plane roared down the runway and escaped into the clouds.

"What do we do now?" Jay asked me.

"Feed them."

"And the girl?" Jay asked, but I had no answer. We'd never dealt with a human powerful enough to frighten God.

***

Anat found me that evening. I was unable to track her on the Island. Even the angels couldn't find her as they combed the forest surrounding the campground. The children were settling into their cabins and I lazily swung a tetherball around a pole. Anat emerged from the path leading to the mountain. She walked directly to me, but her eyes stayed on the ground before her.

"Welcome back," I called.

"Why am I here?" she asked, brusque as she had been on Earth.

"God brought you to the Island."

"As a reward?"

"An experiment," I said.

Anat met my eyes, then looked to a small group of boys leaving a cabin and walking to the lake. They paused when they saw Anat. I motioned them back to their cabin and they complied quickly.

"What's happened to me?" Anat asked.

"You are happening to you. This Island works differently than Earth. Most children don't discover this until much later, but you? I am not sure. I've never seen someone like you before. You are very special."

Anat frowned at this. Her eyes wanted to cry, but she was too proud to let them. She detested looking weak in front of others.

"What now?" Anat asked.

"Do you feel comfortable staying in a cabin with a few other girls?"

"No."

"That's okay."

I looked to the sky and motioned to an angel. Anat followed my eyes, but could not see the great, winged beast approaching. I turned to Anat.

"You missed dinner, so go fix yourself something to eat. I will figure out your sleeping arrangements."

Anat nodded as I pointed her toward the mess hall.

"And thank you for coming back."

"Don't touch me again," she responded coldly.

"I won't, I promise."

Anat turned to me, managed a slim smile, still fighting back tears. She turned and strode to the mess hall. I then told the angel to prepare Cabin Zero.

How To Properly Manage A Young Empire
Part 2

The Mayor woke in her own bed, town elders chatting softly in the hall, Hillary planted on a chair facing the bed while scribbling in a notebook. The Mayor leaned up. A searing pain shot through her skull, nearly sending her back into unconsciousness. Hillary was at the bedside, holding The Mayor's hand and gently nudging her back down to the pillow.

The pain was a blasting siren, a jackhammer, and scorching blood boiling in her brain. Confused, nauseous colors sparked in her eyes. A deep sweat rose across her skin. Then she slept.

The Mayor woke again, finding the sunrise appearing through the mouth of the cave. The pain evaporating like a morning mist burned away by the sun. She saw a face above her, her focus sharpening.

"Good morning," I said to her as I leaned close and placed my hand against her scalp. I'd crossed the lake to find out what happened and, hopefully, to defuse a potential war.

She slapped my hand away. She gingerly sat up against the headboard, then grimaced when pain sprang up from her right knee. She pulled up the sheets to see her purpled and swollen knee cap. Even on the Island, some injuries took time to heal.

She lowered the sheets and examined the faces of the town elders surrounding the bed.

She was humiliated and furious. She briefly considered sending them all to the ovens and beginning anew.

Her eyes rested on Hillary, with that notebook full of pencil scratches and secrets. Hillary would have to go.

"Where is he?" The Mayor asked, her mouth dry, mucky, like

the slime left from a dried lake bed.

"Gone," I answered.

"Send your angels to find him," The Mayor shot back.

"We don't do that."

The Mayor scanned the room, finding Walter, the arms engineer.

"Get back to work."

Walter traded a quick look with an imposing, but measured man who served as New Wichita's lone judge. The Mayor found the judge to be difficult, but also loyal enough. The judge nodded, whispered to Walter, and they left the room together.

The Mayor looked at me. "If you aren't going to help us, then you aren't welcome within our borders."

"I can accept that, but let me offer you a little advice," I said. "Going to war with Simon or the Engineers is not going to work out for you."

"Simon invaded our borders," she said, then took a few moments to clear her mouth and swallow hard. "It is our right to defend ourselves."

"True, but don't act hastily. I will talk to Simon. Give me time."

"Go."

I stood from the bed and left without a word. The room remained silent as they heard my footsteps exit the house, then the door shutting behind me.

"How bad is it?" The Mayor asked.

Rabia walked through the room and sat down on the bed, her eyes avoiding the Mayor's.

"City Hall is gone," Rabia said. "There was some damage to other buildings and there is a fairly sizable hole in the cavern ceiling, but Hauan thinks it'll hold as long as we leave it alone. I would not be comfortable doing any more developing in downtown until we can fully assess the cavern's stability."

"On the upside, downtown has a sunroof," the master brewer said. The joke failed to land and the brewer resettled, uneasily, in his seat.

"Will God allow it?" The Mayor asked.

"Bali said it wouldn't be a problem, for now," Rabia said.

The Mayor eased back against the pillow and closed her eyes. "Good, maybe that brat did us a favor. How many people did we lose?"

"Three are still unaccounted for," Rabia said. "Hauan seems confident they will be found soon, though."

"What do we do?" the brewer asked.

The Mayor sighed, her eyes still closed. The pain was gone, but she was still left with a hazy fog drifting through her thoughts.

"We need a meeting with the Engineers, immediately," she said.

"They won't help us assassinate the boy," Rabia said. "We have tried before."

"Everything is negotiable. We just haven't found their price, yet."

The Girl Who Doomed God
Part 3

Anat watched the moon from the porch swing of God's cabin while the rest of the campground slept. She'd showed no interest in associating with the other campers, instead spending the day locked away inside Cabin Zero. Well past the moment when the last light was extinguished, she emerged and toured the campground alone. She finally claimed God's porch swing and none had opposed her.

If she cried at any point, I hadn't seen it. I could only guess at her thoughts. She had locked herself away from me in a way I'd never experienced. Not on the Island. Not in the Wilderness. Not even on Earth. She's not the first mind I couldn't slip into. God's mind was an impenetrable fortress, Simon's was a shadow, but Anat's was a heavy, oak door that would crack open at times, then be slammed back shut before I could slide through.

Footsteps broke her gaze and she looked over at a figure approaching from the forest. She straightened on the swing, her feet touching the floor to stop the swaying seat. She watched a boy approach, alone, with a quiet smile. He wore the same shorts and t-shirt as the other campers, but she didn't remember him from the airfield. He didn't speak as he walked around the cabin towards the front porch. His eyes remained fixed on hers.

"Leave me alone," Anat said.

"My name is Simon."

Anat didn't respond. She rose from the swing and stood stiffly, her arms folded across her chest.

"I've heard about you," he continued, nearing the porch steps.

"Stop."

"Why?" Simon asked, still approaching slowly.

"I don't want to hurt you." Heat beget to build in her chest, flowing out of her heart. Simon winced as the waves hit him. He placed his foot on the first step of the porch.

The heat spiked. Behind her, a sign reading "Take Your Shoes Off" tacked to the front door began smoldering.

"Please, stop." Anat stepped backwards away from Simon, her legs bumping against the porch swing.

"I won't hurt you."

A dried leaf that had been trapped in a corner of the porch erupted into flames.

"But I will hurt you," Anat said. "Just leave me alone."

"You won't hurt me," Simon replied, his voice calm, his smile kind.

The chains on the porch swing glowed red. Simon took another step forward. Flames leapt from the siding and porch, climbing the outside walls of the cabin and spreading across the roof.

But the heat did not touch Simon. He stepped forward.

The chains of the porch swing melted and snapped, sending the flaming seat clattering to the floor. Flames roared around the two children. Simon stood only inches away from Anat.

"I won't hurt you," Simon repeated, his eyes locked on hers. "You are a goddess. I want to worship you."

Anat's glare faded into something between hope and fear.

"Who are you?" she asked as the inferno brightened the night sky.

The eyes of children appeared from windows and front doors, watching the flames. Across the lake, the fisherman stood in their boats and gazed at the distant campground.

Behind Simon, a crowd of children was beginning to congregate, watching the cabin burn. I was sprinting across the campground. A scream drew her eyes above where an angel swept toward the fire, but was turned back by the intense heat. It left a trail of smoke as it flew back to the lake where it plunged into the water.

"Please, leave me alone," Anat said. The house was beginning to collapse, the porch floor buckling everywhere but underneath Anat and Simon.

"Behind this cabin is a trail. Follow that trail to a waterfall. Across that waterfall, I will be waiting for you."

"Who are you?" Anat asked again, tears in her eyes.

"I am a god. Together, we will rule this island."

I Cannot Die
Part 6

I am looking for a new beginning. That is what I see in the blackness beyond this realm. Not a void, not an absence of God's light, but rather a rebirth. There are times that I feel a great eye on me, shielded behind a curtain, peering deep into our universe. It watches me, waiting, just as curious about me as I am about it.

When I met my brother in the desert during his brief life on Earth, I was furious with what God asked me to do. Playing games with the hearts of men again. If I wanted, I could have broken my brother's resolve.

But I didn't. His destiny was to win; mine was to lose.

I said the lines God demanded of me. But my brother stood firm. I am glad that he did, for I also believed that there was a need for forgiveness.

I was tempted myself that day—tempted to unveil the ending of my brother's life to him while he withered in a desert. If I had told Jesus that he was going to die on a cross, abandoned by God to become a symbol, he would have turned.

I know this for a fact. God would have punished Jesus, then He would have punished Man. I would have been left untouched, but forever shunned by my Father. A child eternally scolded for doing his job a little too well.

God does not like to lose.

Martha The Believer
Part 4

Torrential rains arrived the morning after God had fled the Island. Willow's drenched hood clung to her face, practically suffocating her as she struggled with the last pup tent. Yet she did not call for help from the others, who remained safely inside their own shelters. Willow understood when she was not wanted. She was already making plans to leave in the morning.

Martha lay curled up in her sleeping bag, shivering as she listened to the wind slapping against the tent fabric. Martha felt the absence of God like the empty static of a record player at the end of side B. She knew it was a moment for strong faith. But she didn't crave God. She craved the arms of a man instead.

Any man.

Not sex, just warmth.

Perhaps a little sex.

But she would not bow to temptation that easily. Instead, she clung to her bitterness, trapping it inside the sleeping bag and pressing it against her chest. It was a safe, simple emotion. It would protect her much better than any man she ever met.

Including God. That part she only felt, never dared to say, even in her mind.

The storm passed and the afternoon sun burned through the fading storm clouds. Martha rolled wearily from her bag and unzipped the tent.

Fallen branches littered the ground. A collapsed tent was propped up just enough to allow its occupant to breathe.

Willow, Martha guessed. Cheyenne crawled out from another tent and looked over at Martha. Then she noticed Willow's ruined tent a few steps away from hers and started over to help.

Martha shook her head. Cheyenne returned to her own tent and disappeared inside.

They'd made camp within the forest, a hundred feet from the pit where the legless and armless man still remained, impaled. Martha could barely see him through the trees. He had a shred of white fabric wrapped over his head like a bonnet to protect him from the rain.

Willow, Martha guessed again.

"Come on out, we're all still alive," Martha called to the others.

They awoke roughly with lots of hushed mutterings, not accustomed to outdoor life. One by one, the tents birthed believers. All but Willow had abandoned their burkas. At the sight of the others in their shorts and t-shirts, Willow timidly pulled off her hood. She swept her hair in front of her face, which she was sure was still disease-ridden and ugly.

It wasn't. It was among the loveliest faces to ever appear on the Island. Martha knew resenting a woman for her beauty must qualify as a deadly sin, but she had neither time nor energy to find peace with the inequities of Willow's physical gifts. She told herself that she preferred faith and intellect to good looks, but that didn't feel true.

"Good morning," a distant voice called.

Martha spun to face a cluster of trees. A dozen men and women approached.

"Behind me!" Martha growled and her followers quickly fell into a wedge pattern behind their leader.

"Don't be scared," a tall black woman called. She wore a sundress that accentuated her arms and legs like long, sinewy branches. "We are friends from New Wichita."

"I don't know what that is," Martha replied.

"It's a godly town," the woman said, motioning for her group to stop. "The only true civilization in the Wilderness. Our mayor would like to meet with you and your people."

"Why?" Martha asked.

The woman hesitated. She looked over at a brute of a man standing next to her. He nodded his head.

The woman looked back to Martha. "Simon. We are afraid that Simon will corrupt our people. We need strength, and we understand that is what you are best at."

Martha's face lit up with a smile. She wanted to reply with a simple "yes," but that would have been prideful.

"With God's grace."

"Follow us," the tall woman said. She turned and led the group back into the forest.

"And good morning to you, CeeCee!" the legless, armless man called from his pike.

"Good morning to you," the tall woman responded with a polite smile. "That's a nice hat you have there."

The legless, armless man chuckled as he peered up from beneath the brim of his bonnet.

"It'll keep the crows off," he said, then glanced back at Willow. She rewarded him with a perfect smile.

The Woman's Severed Head

She watched Petrov fuss with pots in the kitchen as she rested on a wet towel, slowly absorbing the moisture. Pain raged around the raw meat of her neck and, sometimes, she swore she could feel her fingertips. She closed her eyes and imagined having a body again, reaching out and dipping her fingers into Petrov's hair, feeling the loose curls and the bumpy scalp underneath.

He would turn and grab her by the thighs, pulling her up and against him, her legs locking around his waist. They would kiss with a frenzy. A mad release.

She opened her eyes. Her face felt flushed. The pain had receded. She smiled as he glanced over at her. It came off crooked and unpracticed. She had never been much of a smiler.

"Smile with your eyes," her mother would tell her when the family posed for photos. As a young, awkward, and brainy girl, she had thought it foolish nonsense.

Now, as a severed head, she had nothing to lose. She smiled with her eyes the next time Petrov looked at her. He paused, a saucepan in his hand, watching her with an expression of amused curiosity.

"May I paint you tonight?" Petrov asked.

Her smile widened, spreading across her face like a flower in bloom. She blinked once for "yes" and Petrov dipped his head in an appreciative bow.

Then he turned from her and placed the saucepan on the stove. She looked away. She still felt a touch restless, but she was more content than she might have expected she could ever be, with or without a body.

Petrov poured sugar into the saucepan and lit the burner.

She clicked her teeth together to get the painter's attention.

He half-turned to her. She aimed her eyes at the saucepan.

"I have been thinking about your situation," Petrov said. "You must eat to survive. I can keep you nourished like a potted plant, allowing your roots to soak up nutrients from the pillow, but your mouth needs a reason to exist."

The painter turned back to the saucepan, stirring slowly. Hints of smoke wafted through the air. She recognized the scent of caramel. Petrov opened a jar and reached in with a spoon to retrieve a dollop of butter. He flicked it from his spoon down into the sizzling pan, then removed the pan from the burner.

"I do not understand how you are alive," Petrov continued, lifting the woman and her pillow off the counter and walking her to the table. "I am thinking of a myriad of problems, like how you are processing oxygen without lungs, how you are processing vitamins and nutrients without a stomach, but the Island changes all of us."

Petrov lowered her onto the table. He returned to the saucepan and poured caramel onto a plate. He waved his hand over the caramel as he brought it to the table and placed it near the woman. She looked at the thick sauce, the color of a worn penny, and remembered the taste vividly. Crème Brûlée. Ice cream sundaes. Sticky popcorn. The candies that pulled her fillings out, enraging her father.

Petrov walked to the kitchen and poured water from a pitcher into a crude coffee cup. He grabbed a spoon, then returned to the table and sat down next to her.

"What I am trying to tell you is there will be much trial and error," Petrov said. "So, you can be patient with me?"

The woman was now certain she was in the full flush of love, and her eyes expressed this with more clarity than words ever could. A tear surfaced, all her head could manage. There would have been a waterfall, had she possessed the resources.

"Is that a 'yes'?"

She blinked once. The tear rolled down her cheek. She smiled with her eyes.

Petrov slowly tipped the cup against her lips. "Just a little bit, to wake your tongue," he whispered, his other hand gently bracing her head.

A small stream of water rolled through her mouth. She held it there and her tastebuds sprouted immediately to life. The flavor spread across her soft palate, so vivid even her teeth seemed to hum with vitality.

"This water comes from a very special place," Petrov said. "I brought some home with me. I did not know exactly why until this moment."

The water was absorbed quickly by her parched mouth yet the energy remained. She aimed her eyes at the cup and Petrov lifted it once more to her lips, tilting it just enough to allow a small sip.

She rolled the moisture throughout her mouth greedily. She pointed her eyes to the caramel. Petrov dipped the tip of the spoon into the caramel and brought it to his own lips to ensure it wasn't too hot.

"Just right," he said. He dipped the spoon deeper into the caramel, lifted it, and brought it to her lips. She opened her mouth, her eyes steady on Petrov.

The warm, rich, slightly smoky sweetness spread out along her taste buds. She closed her eyes, feeling euphoria sweep throughout her head, sparking all the way from her scalp to her phantom toes.

A violent clanging startled them both.

Petrov looked across the kitchen toward the hall that led to the blast door. He lay down the spoon and sighed.

"I will just be a moment," he said, then rose and strode from the kitchen.

The woman salivated like a dog as she stared at the puddle of caramel cooling before her on the plate. She felt her phantom fingertips again, reaching. She heard Petrov throw the lock and swing the heavy door open.

No conversation. Perhaps she heard the faint laughter of a child, but she couldn't be sure.

She returned her focus to the plate. Outside the bunker, Petrov watched a mushroom cloud tumble up into the sky.

***

An hour later she had joined Petrov outside. She watched from a workbench as he stared at a backpack lying in the grass in front of him.

"Would you be willing to ride inside a backpack?" Petrov asked, not looking at her initially. When he finally turned his face to her, she emphatically blinked No!

Petrov shrugged. He stood, formed his hands in the general shape of the woman's head and moved them about his torso and shoulders, measuring. He paced for a while, his eye always on the backpack.

"On my shoulder, on my chest, or on my back?" he asked, then looked at the head.

She wasn't sure how to answer.

"Sorry." He moved his hands in the shape of her head to his chest. "You would be facing forward."

He tilted his hands around, but kept them at his chest. "You would be looking up at me. Like riding in a baby sling."

He turned around and moved his arms behind his back. "You would be looking behind me."

He turned back to her, moving his hands to his shoulder. "You would see what I see."

She blinked yes, excited to have her cheek close to his.

"On my shoulder?" Petrov verified. She blinked YES!

"Okay," he said and set to work. "I do not like the idea of taking you with me because it will be dangerous, but I am not sure how long you could last on your own. For now, we are never apart, you and I."

He retrieved a knife and began ripping up the backpack.

"This will be our first adventure," Petrov continued.

She loved that he said "first."

Yulia Creates So Many Lovely Things

Yulia enjoyed playing with me, punishing my encroachments into her mind with blasts of color, swirling and dancing. She sent me flashes of senseless and beautiful movement like the tumbling falls of snowflakes into shimmering water that waltzed with river rocks.

She was not the most powerful of the Engineers, but she was the most fun, covering her memories behind a beautiful mess of confusion. If God was a fortress, Simon was a shadow, and Anat was an oak door, then Yulia was a rain forest.

I remember her rich, Slavic accent that followed her family to the USA. And I remember when she shed it, adopting in its place a crisp tone—more neutral, more professional, more First World. It had broken her mother's heart to hear her speak with so little flair, but she understood it was important for Yulia to excel in the West.

Yulia was tall and lean, with sharp features and a chin she held high. Like the photos of her grandmother, a prima ballerina who had survived the brutal era of Stalin. Yulia was not a seamstress by trade, but she understood and coveted fashion. When she was cast away to the Wilderness, she found her new skills in great demand from a people exiled from God, all with the same drab shorts and t-shirts. They came to Yulia looking for something new. Any fashion, any fabric, any color. If an exile could pay, Yulia could deliver.

Yulia counted herself as an Engineer, but she traded with the Americans. She did not want to roam naked and wild across the Wilderness, so the Americans built her a cabin near the lake. Shielded by a canopy above, she spent most of her time alone, awaiting the next paying visitor.

And that next visitor was The Mayor of New Wichita. Yulia heard her limping toward the cabin with the aid of a cane. The ground was still soft from the rains, and The Mayor was struggling with the mud. Behind her, a young man carried a large bag of clothing, his penance for being found with Tommy in The Mayor's bed. Yulia had picked up this last bit of gossip from New Wichita's budding journalist who'd come by for a fitting and to dish about the explosion.

Though Yulia bartered in work, product, and resources, it was gossip for which she lusted most. Particularly when it concerned the beautiful man with the ocean eyes. She adored Tommy, how free he was. Even more than the Engineers. Haunted? Yes, but all valuable treasures are cursed.

The richness of the beautiful boy's memory yielded me a brief view into her mind. She felt me leap into her imagination, searching for the last time Tommy visited her cabin.

A burst of color, fiery and enraged, flooded my vision. With a breathy and seductive "Tsk, tsk" from Yulia, I was expelled once more from her thoughts.

It was the game we played. Into her mind, out of her mind. Into my mind, out of my mind. I would love her if she wasn't so frightening.

Yulia stepped out of her cabin and waited for The Mayor and her lackey.

"Good morning, Katherine, my love," Yulia called.

The Mayor wore a delicate Bohemian sundress and silk ballet flats instead of the usual power suit. Yulia had created the outfit upon the Mayor's request.

"Even a professional woman must remember she will always be, in some way, a little girl," Yulia had told The Mayor, who had blushed in a fit of anger and vulnerability.

The Mayor wore the sundress today with equal defiance, showing both strength and femininity, and Yulia adored her for it. Coupled with Yulia's abhorrence of The Mayor's cruelty, the women could be both potent lovers and fierce enemies.

"Yulia, you are lovely as always," The Mayor called with a plasticized smile that looked almost warm.

"You have lucked into more treasure?"

"Yes," The Mayor replied. She seemed to have no interest in elaborating.

Yulia met the lackey's gaze, but he quickly dropped his eyes away. He still wore the earthy brown, pin-striped shorts and dark green, short-sleeve shirt he'd had on since he traded his tent for it a year ago.

A simple design for a simple man.

In the doorway, Yulia stepped aside and motioned for them to enter the cabin. "Off with your shoes," she said. "I can't abide mud on my floors."

Her wondrous eyebrows arched as she stared at the lackey. He managed only a brief, sidewards glance as he kicked off his sneakers. His face flushed as he passed by. She could smell his fear and arousal.

The bag landed on the cabin floor with a whomp like an exhausted dog flopping down on his bed. There were no other doors or inside walls, just a wide open space of about forty by sixty feet. A large oaken work table dominated the middle of the room, and numerous chests filled with fabric were pushed against the walls. Wooden wardrobes hid Yulia's own collection, then a simple kitchen tucked into the back.

There were no scissors, thread, needles or other tools of a normal seamstress. Just the worktable. After gossip, old fabric was her next favorite item. As The Mayor opened the bag to reveal a pile of clothes, Yulia remembered every shirt, every skirt, every belt she had created. Having the clothing returned to her was to have the secrets they had gathered in their travels unlocked. In that bag was a pile of spies, mute to everyone else on the Island but her.

The Mayor nodded for the lackey to leave. He hustled to the door, but Yulia put her hand on his chest and leaned her face close to his.

"Aren't you due for a change of clothes, my boy?" Yulia asked.

"Later," The Mayor called. "I am in a hurry."

"There is always time," Yulia insisted, her fingernail tracing the lackey's chest.

"Everett," The Mayor snapped. "That will be all."

"Yes, ma'am," the lackey answered. His nervous hand lifted to Yulia's, paused a moment as if approaching a viper, then swatted Yulia's hand away. He escaped out of the cabin, slamming the door behind him.

Yulia watched him through the window. Everett, once a wilting rich boy from Connecticut, was now a wilting chef from New Wichita.

"Have you washed Everett and Tommy from your sheets yet?" Yulia asked.

The Mayor didn't answer. Yulia walked to the bag and pulled it open.

"Where did you get these clothes from, Katherine?" Yulia asked.

"I came upon them," she replied.

Yulia ran her fingers through the clothes, remembering their creation. Hip-hugging jeans, lightly embroidered, a satin blouse. Carpenter pants, thin flannel top. The recent exile laughed at the self-conscious Polo shirt and slacks because it looked like what his father would wear. The father who never understood. Yet the exile adored the clothes and the way it framed his shoulders and chest. She saw the last moments the clothes had touched their owners.

The heat.

The blood.

Her fingers recoiled.

"Where are they?" Yulia asked, glaring at the Mayor.

"Does it matter?"

Yulia looked back down into the bag.

"No, it doesn't."

"Good. I have a meeting in an hour," The Mayor said. "I need something formal Elegant but not too showy. Something black and powerful."

Yulia kicked over the bag, watched the garments pour out.

"Something new, please," The Mayor said, her voice trying to be strong.

"Power is in the past, Katherine," Yulia said, grabbing the blouse and the carpenter pants. She tossed them onto the work table.

"Do you need to measure me first?"

"Have you gotten fatter?" Yulia shot back.

The Mayor took a moment too long to answer. She blushed. "No."

"Then I can probably wing it."

Yulia spread the clothes out on the table. She closed her eyes and placed her palms on the fabric. Amber light glowed from her hands, whimsical lines of smoke danced up from her fingertips, tracing upward to the thatched roof. The fabric knitted itself together among the rising flames that burnt its colors to a coal black. The light enveloped the clothes and Yulia's hands.

Yulia opened her eyes and faced The Mayor. The light dimmed. She lifted her palms away and then swiped them together, as if ridding her skin of the soil of hard labor.

Yulia stepped away and The Mayor retrieved the new creation, a suit jacket and modest dress with a cut that was flattering, but not so tight as to be unseemly.

"I was thinking a pantsuit, something more masculine," The Mayor said.

Yulia did not respond.

The Mayor limped to a pair of full-length mirrors tucked into the corner of the room. She set her cane aside and gingerly peeled off her sundress.

"I am keeping the rest of the clothes," Yulia announced.

The Mayor paused, the dress in hand. She turned her face so Yulia could not see her anger, then continued to step into the dress while holding onto a nearby chair, gritting her teeth at the pain in her knee.

She lifted the dress over her shoulders. Yulia walked over and zipped her up in back, then helped her lace her arms into the jacket.

"There. Power and confidence," Yulia whispered into The Mayor's ear as they both looked at the reflection. "No need for a false front of manhood to wield authority. You are a woman, and people will follow because they know you are certain. And you are wearing the bones of your enemies."

The Mayor glanced at Yulia's reflection.

"I can trust you with this secret?" The Mayor asked.

"Yes." Yulia's leaned in toward The Mayor's cheek, her lips pressing against the skin. "We are friends and friends keep secrets."

Perspiration beaded to the surface of The Mayor's face. She eased Yulia away.

"It is absolutely stifling in here," The Mayor said, retrieving her cane. "You should open a window."

Inside The Mayor's new clothes, the heat rose.

"I am good with secrets," Yulia continued. "As discreet as a severed head."

The Mayor straightened. Her fingers tightened against the cane, the sweat now dripping from her chin.

"How many ovens do you have now?" Yulia asked.

The Mayor grabbed the jacket to rip it off, but a burst of heat overwhelmed her. Gasping, she collapsed to the floor, her face dark red.

Yulia stepped over the wilted Mayor and walked back to her table. She began picking through the rest of the clothes.

"How many ovens, my love?"

"Seven," The Mayor said, weakly.

"And these three, where are they now?"

"Petrov," The Mayor muttered, unconsciousness approaching.

Yulia walked back to The Mayor, then lowered to a knee. Yulia leaned over and her fingers traced The Mayor's flushed face.

"You will never bring me clothes like these again," Yulia whispered. "Or you will be sent to Petrov as well."

Yulia took a moment to watch the woman, to measure the effect of her words. Yulia stood up.

"Take off your clothes," Yulia ordered, turning from The Mayor and returning to her work table. "I have thought of something better for you."

The Mayor's flush evaporated and she took in a long, heavy breath. She rolled to her belly, pushed herself up with her elbows, and sat up. She brushed her hair back from her face. She leaned over to her cane, then grunted from her aching knee as she pushed up onto her feet.

"One day we will destroy you and your coven of witches," The Mayor said.

"Perhaps," Yulia responded lightly. "But not today. Now give me your clothes. All of them."

Yulia Creates So Many Lovely Things
Part 2

Emerald was the color of Yulia's most devastating love. The green of poison, of tree frogs, of delicate boas that crush with their embrace.

It was a sporadic affair with a journalist who'd never known a woman so beautiful. He'd bought her one present during their short, explosive affair. It was a small perfume bottle shaped like an emerald green fairy. He'd found it on a shipwreck. The cap had been lost long before, but the bottle itself had only suffered a tiny crack on a wing.

When she touched it, she imagined him touching her in the way only he could. Reverence. Like a monument to an ancient goddess for whom men ripped out their own hearts and tossed them, still beating and spewing blood, at the statue's feet. And he did, espousing devotion, absorbing her body for hours at a time before sending her worn and exhausted back to her husband.

They used each other, as all lovers do, and that was part of the play. She considered loving him properly, leaving her husband, building a new life. But he disappeared. A man who left her was a rarity and the rejection stunned her.

She did not mourn. Women of Yulia's cut did not mourn men. Instead she got angry, and no matter how many other lovers came and went following the journalist, she never let go of that anger.

Yulia watched Billy and Sophia sleep inside a single sleeping bag. She sat at the opening of their tent, moonlight pouring in around her, silhouetting her body beneath the silk robe she wore. Yulia wasn't sure that she'd loved the journalist or anyone in her life enough to sleep so tightly knit together.

Billy rolled to his side, took a deep breath. His eyes opened heavily, focusing on empty space for a moment. He then noticed Yulia. He took a sharp breath in, locking his eyes on her. His hand drifted toward a hunting knife, but Yulia shook her head.

Billy glanced over at Sophia, who still slept. He sat up slowly, putting one hand on her hip, then looking up at Yulia.

"What do you want?" Billy whispered.

"To show you and your beautiful bride your place on the Island."

Yulia rose and stepped away from the tent. She looked over her shoulder at Billy. After a long moment of contemplation, Billy leaned over Sophia. "We have a visitor," he whispered.

Sophia rolled onto her back, yawned.

"Tell whoever it is to go away," Sophia whispered.

"She's one of the Engineers," Billy said.

Sophia hesitated, then sat up in her sleeping bag. Sophia strained to focus her sleepy eyes. Once she recognized Yulia, she sighed and shook her head.

"Let's go," Sophia said. "Bring your knife."

***

The night sky was starless behind a thin veil of clouds that tumbled and stirred like beasts of burden, unsettled and aimless in the absence of their master.

"God has left us again," Yulia said. "He left on His little plane. So easily startled."

With that, Yulia turned and led the couple through the woods. Billy's fingers tapped against the knife strapped to his belt. His other hand clutched Sophia's.

It felt early in the morning to Sophia, perhaps four a.m. A faint morning mist swirled with the wind and draped the trees like ghostly veils. The air felt heavy as if another storm was coming. She listened for the frogs. When bad weather approached, their croaks were loud and urgent, like a mother beckoning her children home. Sophia didn't hear that urgency, though. Just the soft flirtatious chirping of hopeful lovers.

A small, yellow light peeked through the branches. Artificial light. Billy guessed it was a kerosene lamp. Soon a window could be seen, the lamp glowing proud through the woods. Billy thought of the dire warnings of the Wilderness and why Yulia seemed so unafraid. As they neared, Billy made out the details of the log cabin. A little smaller than God's and with a sod roof. It was buffered by flower and vegetable gardens along the outside. Yulia led them to the porch, opened the front door, and waved them inside.

Billy wrapped his arm around Sophia's waste, holding her still at the steps. "Who else is in there?" he asked.

"It will just be us," Yulia answered, a subtle, sensual tone that made Sophia's skin prickle.

"What do you want from us?" Sophia asked.

"To help you," Yulia said, not bothering to hide the hunger in her smile. "And to have you help me, in turn."

"You lay a hand on us, I will kill you," Billy warned.

"I will lay my hands on both of you," Yulia said. "But not exactly in the way you think. I am not your friend. This is not charity, but you need me far more than I need you."

"Who are you?" Sophia asked.

"I am a seamstress. I am going to make you new clothes. I am going to offer you advice that you desperately need. Then I will ask one thing of you in return."

"What if we say no?" Sophia asked.

"Then you will say no," Yulia said. "Please take off your shoes. I can't abide mud on my floors."

Sophia led Billy up the steps, then she pulled off one shoe at a time, using Billy's shoulder for balance. Billy kicked off his shoes. Yulia motioned them inside. Sophia took Billy's hand as Yulia followed them in and closed the door behind them.

Inside, the cabin was dimly lit by the lamp, but clear enough to know that it held few secrets. Sophia looked across the large wardrobes standing along the walls like sentries. Clothes were scattered across a big work table.

Yulia crossed the room with effortless grace, like smoke that moves along a floor and touches nothing but itself. She walked to the windowsill where the lamp glowed. She lifted it from the window and carried it to the center of the room, shadows shifting ominously with the moving light.

"My name is Yulia. I am the only Engineer you can ever find. The others only find you. Unlike my brethren, I enjoy being a part of commerce and society and the lower members of the species."

"Is that how you see us?" Sophia asked. "Lower?"

Yulia rewarded the question with a smile. "No. Your group's arrival has been one of the most curious things to happen on the Island since I have been here."

"And how long is that?" Billy asked.

"A long time—years, decades," Yulia answered. "I was part of the third group. That was back when we spent more time in the campground, instead of getting exiled within months like you and your friends."

"Is that why you're older, you and the rest of the Engineers?" Billy asked.

Yulia feigned a wounded expression. "Tsk, tsk, Billy. It is not polite to discuss a woman's age." Then she turned her eyes to Sophia. "You must teach him better manners, my dear. But no, we do not appear older due to years, but rather to enlightenment.

We do not cling to youth like the others because we do not need it. We derive our worth from our power."

"You still look much younger than the other Engineers," Sophia replied.

"Well, I am not quite enlightened enough to discard vanity."

"What do you know about the explosion?" Billy asked.

"That was the lower members of the species doing what they do best."

"What do you mean?" Sophia asked.

Yulia smiled as an adult does to a curious, naive child, then walked to the work table and faced the couple.

"Take off your clothes and lay them on the table," she said.

Billy and Sophia didn't move.

"No," Sophia said.

Yulia tapped her nails on the table.

"Please," Yulia said, a degree sharper.

"We don't need new clothes," Billy said. "These are just fine."

Yulia threw her head back and laughed, a witch-like cackle that made Billy jump.

"No, they are not just fine. They are atrocious and ill-fitting and embarrassing. I have seen thousands of naked bodies in my life. I am more interested in your clothing than I am in your flesh. I will even close my eyes if it will make you feel better."

Billy glanced at Sophia.

"This is the cost of answers," Yulia said. "Unlike the favor I will ask of you, new clothes are not negotiable."

Yulia pointed to her eyes, then closed them tight and waved her hands away as if performing magic.

Sophia took a deep breath and lifted her shirt over her head. She looked at Billy before unlatching her bra. He closed his eyes too, obediently. Sophia unbuttoned her shorts and stepped out of them. Then she carried the pile of clothes over to the table where Yulia, eyes still closed, too them and straightened them out on the table.

Upon feeling the bra, Yulia paused. She frowned.

"Come to me," Yulia said, holding up her hands, reaching out for Sophia's.

"Why?" Sophia asked.

"I need to measure you," Yulia said. "I promise it will not hurt."

With timid steps, Sophia rounded the table and took Yulia's hands.

With the tips of her fingers, Yulia passed electric warmth to Sophia's palms. Sophia jerked back.

"I'm sorry, did that hurt?" Yulia asked, playfully.

Sophia studied the woman, Yulia's hands still held out. Sophia took her hands again, the warmth emerging in Sophia's palms, sparking her nerves, traveling up the veins of her forearms to her chest, catching Sophia's breath.

Yulia moved Sophia's hands down to Sophia's side. Yulia traced her fingertips along Sophia's arm. Goosebumps rose. Hormonal burst sparked in Sophia's mind. She moaned.

"Sophia?" Billy called, his eyes still closed.

"She is fine," Yulia replied. "Keep your eyes closed like a good boy."

Yulia leaned closer to Sophia, her fingertips exploring Sophia's chest, never quite touching, but near enough for Sophia to feel the heat emanating. Sophia's breaths were short and conflicted.

"You lie with him every night," Yulia whispered into Sophia's ear, electricity leaping from her lips to Sophia's earlobe. "Yet always separated by these filthy clothes."

Sophia opened her mouth to reply, but the glow passing through her neurons kept her silent.

"Billy is not the other men. He will protect you, and you will protect him. You should not hide from love, Sister Sophia. It will deliver you."

Sophia felt tears stream from her eyes, as much from sorrow as from the electricity passing along her thighs and hips. Close. Too close.

Sophia jerked away, bumping against the table, and held her arms out protectively.

"Sophia?" Billy called.

"I'm okay," Sophia said, but she was still gasping for breath.

"We're done," Yulia said with a smile. "Have your love bring me his clothes."

"No!" Sophia said. "You will not touch him."

"I will have him for a few moments, after which you'll have him for eternity. Or I can take him and never give him back. Your choice, my love."

Sister Sophia
Part 2

A sliver of morning glowed along the outline of the Island's eastern ridge. Billy and Sophia walked through the darkness of the waking forest, wearing new clothes and an uncomfortable silence. Conflicted thoughts like currents passed between them, inching them further and further with every turn of their confused minds.

Sophia wore a knee-length wool skirt with buttons up the front. It would have barely passed in Catholic school. A satin undershirt then a fitted long-sleeved dress shirt, unbuttoned, finished off with calf-length boots.

Billy wore a dark blue, short-sleeved dress shirt with a military cut, tan pants and hiking boots.

"I could make you both into glamorous socialites—ravishing creatures that would shame all other couples on the Island," the Seamstress had told them. "But you want simple, so I will give you simple."

A confusing, warm shiver crossed Sophia's body at the memory of the woman's voice, her presence. Sophia's hand found Billy's.

Since leaving the cabin, Sophia had felt a rising tide of emotion coming on. She was having trouble holding it back. Part of it was anger, but there was something else, something new she'd never felt. Jealousy? Close, but not quite.

She pulled Billy's hand to bring him closer, lacing her hands around his arm, feeling his biceps, taking in his scent. The new clothes carried a fresh, almost laundered fragrance, but beneath was the musk of the man she loved. Her body pressed closer against him.

Small, fluttering lights appeared in the bushes along the trail before them as fireflies awakened at their approach. They glittered, hovering just above the path, as if to light the couple's way.

A bird called. An owl answered. Soft rustlings indicated movement in the brush. Billy noticed it all and noticed that Sophia paid it no mind.

She hugged him closer.

Cat's eyes glowed white in the moonlight, tracking Billy and Sophia. The call of crickets swelled, not loud, just present, like a film score. From high above them, something sang. Birds were now soaring above, gliding down into the trees, finding perches to overlook the scene.

Sophia felt warm. So very warm. He recognized it, the way her fingers tightened against his arm, a finger tracing, examining, straying up under his sleeve.

Billy was trying not to watch her, Sophia knew. He was a gentleman. He knew how to give her space, and he'd done so admirably since they arrived to the Wilderness. Holding her, sleeping next to her, but never pressing, knowing that she was not ready.

Sophia laid her face to his shoulder, breathing him in, tears soaking into the cotton fabric. She saw the lightning bugs, heard the animals, but was not stirred by them. They were stirred by her.

Sophia stopped walking.

"Everything okay?" Billy asked quietly.

Sophia reached for his other hand and pulled him around, stepped into his arms and hugged him with her head against his chest.

"Thank you for not—" she began, but she couldn't finish. She didn't want to think of the Seamstress. She didn't want to say the woman's name. Whatever this moment was, she didn't want to spoil it.

"Of course," Billy answered, kissing her softly on her head. "Of course."

She drew in a heavy breath, a hint of a sob within. She was shaking slightly. She freed a hand to wipe away her tears, but didn't look up at Billy.

"I need you," she said, wrapping her hand back around his waist, looking directly at his chest.

The crickets silenced, the birds settled, and the Wilderness held its breath.

"I need you, too," Billy said. "And I will be here for you forever."

"I need you," she said again. He hugged her closer, resting his face down onto her head.

"I am here."

"Billy," Sophia said, curtly, pulling away and looking up at him. Her reddened eyes were lifted. She smiled. "I need you."

"OK," Billy replied. His eyes widened. "Oh! Need me! Um, now?"

Sophia didn't answer. Instead she just gazed up at him and smiled more broadly. Around them, the orchestra of life resumed its hum. With a quick, sheepish chuckle, Billy lifted Sophia from the ground and into his arms as if carrying her over a threshold. The lightning bugs swept ahead of him, exposing a side trail. He followed them into a darkened cluster of trees. The lights went out and the sounds swelled, hiding the lovers from prying eyes both human and divine. Beneath the shroud, among muffled whispers, forgotten clothing, and heavy breaths, Billy took Sophia in a way every woman should be taken, at least once in their lives.

***

They dressed quickly, giggling and smiling like teenagers. They made a game of pulling each other back into the trees, kissing madly, then peeling away to return to the trail. It took them hours to find their camp, but the time passed quickly.

Upon sighting the first tent, the sun high in the air, prudence finally returned to Sophia's swimming head. She looked down at her new clothes, already messy with grass stains on the skirt.

"What are we going to tell them?" Sophia asked.

"We were accosted by forest bandits?" Billy said with a serious nod. "I fought them off nobly."

Sophia rolled her eyes, then leaned up to kiss him.

"I am less concerned with the state of the clothes than with the fact that they are not the ones we left in."

"An Engineer gave us new clothes," Billy said. "In exchange for a favor. Simple."

"But when they ask for new clothes, too?"

"She will come for them when she is ready. That's what she said."

Sophia bit her lip and looked back toward the campground. She spotted Ossie with a load of firewood. He freed a hand and waved. Billy waved back.

"But when she comes for them," Sophia said. "And she does what she does, they will know that she did that to us and—I just feel very uncomfortable about everything."

Billy pulled her into his arms. She allowed it, but was not as enthusiastic as before. Her mind was at the edge of a spiral, she could feel it.

"I am not sure what to say," Billy whispered. "What happened with her was—scary. I know that is weird to say, but I don't like us being that exposed. As far as what other people think, I simply don't care. As long as I have you, then I am solid."

"And the favor she wants from us?" Sophia asked.

Billy looked back to the path.

"No. Hell no."

Sophia adjusted her head against his chest. She felt better by a degree, but also a little amused at his simplicity. His heart seemed to have a brute momentum, and perhaps she would just allow it to pull her along for awhile, until things seemed simpler.

"If there is anything or anyone I can punch to make this better, let me know," he said.

Sophia laughed, then laced her hand behind his head and pulled him down into a tender, lingering kiss. When they broke apart, she smiled up at him.

"Roger that."

Martha the Believer
Part 5

Lines of workers were clearing away the debris, passing stones from person to person and tossing them to the sides of the cave entrance.

"Stay here and wait for us to come back," CeeCee instructed Martha as she walked ahead to talk to the workers.

So Martha waited, perched upon a fallen log like a queen, the followers silent as they busied themselves with plucked berries and faint whispers. It was the first time Martha had ever been summoned, and she relished it, soaked in the mystery of it. She felt herself changing, evolving.

Martha gazed ahead to New Wichita to wait for the Americans to return for their prized emissary. Martha wasn't sure that "emissary" was the right word, but she liked the way it sounded. She began thinking about how to announce herself as such, or perhaps have a follower do it instead. Yes, she thought, it must be a follower. Leaders only talk to leaders. The followers would be the messengers that dealt with the low-Islanders.

Willow stood and approached Martha.

"Ma'am?" Willow said, but Martha didn't reply. "Ma'am? I am getting hungry. Can I walk back to the pit and get some of the—stuff?"

"Eat of the Earth with the others," Martha said, feeling like she was finding her voice. Very regal, like an emissary.

"But we ain't on Earth," Willow said. April shushed her. Willow ducked her head away from Martha, letting the hair cover her face, then began scanning bushes.

Willow gasped as God materialized from a bursting mist. He approached from the trees. His eyes scanned the cave and the workers buzzing around the damage. He retreated a few steps back into the cover of the trees.

Martha's heart jumped and she struggled to maintain her regal composure. She remained sitting for a moment, then began to stand, but hesitated, sat back down, then stood up quickly.

"Father," Martha called, but it came off less like a dignitary and more like a surprised teenager. "We thought You'd left the Island again."

"I did, but now I am back."

God wore a "Give Blood, Save A Life" t-shirt and an overly starched pair of blue jeans. His brown sunglasses reflected the sunlight in glimmers as tree branches swayed overhead.

"Can I have a moment with Martha?" God asked.

"Yes, Father," April gasped, motioning the others up and leading them away into the trees.

God motioned for Martha to follow him, so she did, but at a very measured, distinguished pace. They followed a trail for a while and found more trees felled by the raining debris. He gestured for her to sit on a log. He sat a few inches away. They both looked ahead.

"I need your help, Martha."

She smiled big, but then swallowed it and focused on piety.

"Of course, Father. Anything."

"I made a mistake."

Martha's face paled. She turned to look at God. He did not return the gaze, so she looked back to the woods.

"This Island, it was a mistake," God continued. "I am an old man now. I knew it and I should have left it alone, but I thought I had one more in Me." He breathed in the smell of pine, allowing the wind to tickle His beard. "I don't," He said.

"But You are eternal, Father. You are our Constant."

"I thought so, too," God replied. "I thought I never aged, never changed, as steady as the stars. But they are not steady either, are they?"

"I don't know, Father. I wasn't good at science."

God chuckled and patted her hand. He had no idea the effect this had on her. He also had no idea that I was watching.

"I know, Martha, I know. I look back now and see how much I changed. I once thought it was the world, the people, life that was in flux. But it was Me. It was always Me. I started out angry and young, wiping out life in tantrums like a toddler wrecking his toys. Then I was bitter and contemplative, a sullen teenage pseudo-intellectual. Then came adulthood, calm, steady, perhaps too distant. Finally, the End."

God removed his hand from Martha's just before she tried to lace her fingers with His.

"I wasn't going to end the world, you know? I'd decided to let humanity play itself out. Judgment Day was supposed to come so much sooner. My Son promised that to the disciples. It was to be within their lifetimes, but they did not act how I thought they would act. I was fascinated by how quickly My Son's words spread, how far His legend grew. I couldn't stop watching. Then the disciples were gone and the church rose. Civilization was forever impacted by My slightest touch, sent spinning like a top, careening off at the slightest tap of the finger. I was dazzled and watched the centuries pass, intervening in only the slightest ways, just to see what happened."

"Why did you end it?" Martha asked.

"Humans were getting too close to Me. They were getting too close to My secrets. I brought the Rapture hastily upon the world, and I did a rather sloppy job with it. I regret much of it. I just didn't have the energy to do it properly. I didn't have my youth."

Martha felt like she was beginning to understand. She pulled the hair back from her face and half-turned on the log to face God. It was her pretty side.

"And the Island?" she asked, her hand moving closer to His.

"Another hasty decision. I was bored and feeling old. I wanted to prove something to Myself, I suppose. I wanted to prove that I was ageless."

"You are, Father!"

God gazed at Martha. He smiled, uncertain.

"Thank you."

"But you are, and you can finish this Island and make it perfect! I just know it!"

"Thank you. That is why I am here. I need you, Martha."

"And I need you!"

God didn't understand what the moment meant, but He could feel it getting away from Him. He suddenly felt very crowded, so He stood up and took a few steps away from Martha.

"As I was saying, I need your help. I want to ask you something."

"Yes!"

Martha leapt to her feet and jumped into God's arms, her legs wrapping around His waist. He staggered backwards until He steadied himself against a tree as she peppered His face with kisses.

"Yes, I will marry you!"

"What?" God asked, trying to dodge her lips.

"We are going to be so happy, Father!"

She pressed her face into His chest as she hugged Him tightly.

"I need to go," God said.

He disappeared and Martha fell to the ground. She rolled onto her back and let out a rapturous shriek. The followers rushed back to her.

"Are you okay?" April asked.

Martha sat up, hair a mess, smile wicked.

"I am going to be the wife of God."

Our Lord In Heaven

God found me at the campground, looking over the cinders of His cabin. He strode up to me without even acknowledging the wreckage of His home.

"I thought you were off in Heaven," I said.

"I was, but I turned back."

"Without your plane?"

"Getting here is easy. Getting out's the problem."

"Isn't that always the way?"

"Yes, well, the plane will be back soon, so never mind that. I need to talk to you about something. I had this idea I wanted to pursue but, um, there was an issue."

I already knew where this was headed, but decided to let it play out naturally. "How so?" I asked as innocently as I could.

God looked to the campers in the distance, then back to me. "I just made a big mistake."

I could smell Martha on Him. It took all my power to keep from laughing in our Creator's face.

I Cannot Die
Part 7

Such memories. Such a life. Such a far away life.

And I see it. There. The end of God's grasp, the very tip of His fingers. I believe I see a light beyond. But I have been smothered in darkness for so long, I cannot even say if my eyes would understand light anymore. Not even if I floated through a supernova.

If that distant twinkle is true, then it is an Other. It is not of God, or at least of my God. I believe I hear a call, like a child calling from across a vast field to a potential playmate. Whether it's imagined or real, this call stirs my heart with memories of my many friends. I can only assume they are all dead now. Some will be doomed. Some will have been reclaimed by the One who forsook me. I miss them all, and I miss the Island.

The light is bright and alive, I am sure of it. I registered a deep chill sweep across my skin. It began at my scalp and crawled across my body until it reached my toes. I am enveloped in cold now. I have left His dominion. His grace. I am cold, but the light twinkles ahead. Something's about to change. I may never be able to tell you what I see. These may be the last thoughts I send you.

But, Simon, be good to them all. Be better than He was to you. It is your kingdom now. I only wish I could see what you have done with it.

Farewell to my friend, the Devil

Oh, Bali. You tourist. I knew your kind, the happy-handed traveler who loved to be scammed. They came in great swarms, millions of joyful moths flapping, flapping, flapping into the glittery inferno of Las Vegas.

You were known as a great deceiver, but I wonder if you ever knew that you were the rube all along. I've known my fair share of demons. They were honest in a way a holy man never could be. All those high-minded promises the clergymen offered but didn't believe. Not a damn one of them.

I'll take a devil every day. I'll favor small selfish lies over the greatest prank played on our poor human race.

Do you remember Olivia from Connecticut? A fresh-out-of-the-package divorcee tossing around her alimony just to show her ex-fella that his car lot empire was being pissed away on fussy cocktails and male hookers.

I told her, our fingers brushing as we leaned over the blackjack table, "I bet you that, by the end of this night, I will have stolen every penny in your bank account and you will be thanking me for it."

Her eyes dazzled, a warm red flush rose in her cheeks—like tells in a poker game, sure signs I had her hooked. Twenty three thousand dollars and seven hours later, I was kissing her in the drop-off lane at the McAarran International Airport. I didn't even leave her enough money to buy lunch while she waited for her flight. She pawned some jewelry while I watched from the car.

It was a virtuosic performance, and we both knew it. She'd come back to Vegas a few times looking for me, but I ducked her. I was never gonna shine like that again. Genius repeated becomes something smaller each time, something paler. A good performer knows when to bow.

Bali. My aimless traveler. My eternal castaway. Floating into another universe, huh? Whoever is on the other side doesn't know what's coming. You're gonna gobble up all their silly birds who've never known a cat like you. They will have no way to protect themselves from God's bastard son. The Prince o' Darkness. The Morningstar.

Then you'll mope cause nobody's got a conscience as big and silly as yours.

I do hope we can continue talking. There is so much to discuss about the Island. I've been buried deep with the affairs of this universe and I've never had time to discern what exactly happened in God's most wonderful failure. The Island still exists, after so much time, but it looks very different. Better, I think.

But let's talk more of the past. Let's discuss the ways the Creator went wrong. It is good for the new boss to understand what went wrong with the old boss, isn't it?

So, my sad devil, let's start from the real beginning. I wanna talk about the exact moment I realized I was more powerful than God.

The Martin & Weinke Continuum

From the escapades of a rock prophet to the global culling of humanity by Mother Nature, the Martin & Weinke Continuum connects standalone novels tracing our stumbling march to the end of civilization and beyond. These satirical, character-focused, and cross-genre stories examine our tenuous perch atop the food chain and what happens when everything else on the planet, both natural and unnatural, decides it's time for humans to be dethroned.

In order of continuity:

- *the dominant hand*
- *Deviants*
- *Pets*
- *Edward & The Island*
- *Edward & The Wilderness*
- *Edward & The Infinite*

www.ingramcontent.com/pod-product-compliance
Lightning Source LLC
Chambersburg PA
CBHW031119020726
47495CB00007B/2260